DEATH BY
Diamonds

ANNETTE BLAIR

BERKLEY PRIME CRIME, NEW YORK

THE BERKLEY PUBLISHING GROUP
Published by the Penguin Group
Penguin Group (USA) Inc.
375 Hudson Street, New York, New York 10014, USA
Penguin Group (Canada), 90 Eglinton Avenue East, Suite 700, Toronto, Ontario M4P 2Y3, Canada
(a division of Pearson Penguin Canada Inc.)
Penguin Books Ltd., 80 Strand, London WC2R 0RL, England
Penguin Group Ireland, 25 St. Stephen's Green, Dublin 2, Ireland (a division of Penguin Books Ltd.)
Penguin Group (Australia), 250 Camberwell Road, Camberwell, Victoria 3124, Australia
(a division of Pearson Australia Group Pty. Ltd.)
Penguin Books India Pvt. Ltd., 11 Community Centre, Panchsheel Park, New Delhi—110 017, India
Penguin Group (NZ), 67 Apollo Drive, Rosedale, North Shore 0632, New Zealand
(a division of Pearson New Zealand Ltd.)
Penguin Books (South Africa) (Pty.) Ltd., 24 Sturdee Avenue, Rosebank, Johannesburg 2196,
South Africa

Penguin Books Ltd., Registered Offices: 80 Strand, London WC2R 0RL, England

This is a work of fiction. Names, characters, places, and incidents either are the product of the author's imagination or are used fictitiously, and any resemblance to actual persons, living or dead, business establishments, events, or locales is entirely coincidental. The publisher does not have any control over and does not assume any responsibility for author or third-party websites or their content.

DEATH BY DIAMONDS

A Berkley Prime Crime Book / published by arrangement with the author

PRINTING HISTORY
Berkley Prime Crime mass-market edition / July 2010

Copyright © 2010 by Annette Blair.
Excerpt from *Skirting the Grave* by Annette Blair copyright © by Annette Blair.
Cover illustration by Kimberly Schamber.
Cover design by Rita Frangie.
Interior text design by Laura K. Corless.

All rights reserved.
No part of this book may be reproduced, scanned, or distributed in any printed or electronic form without permission. Please do not participate in or encourage piracy of copyrighted materials in violation of the author's rights. Purchase only authorized editions.
For information, address: The Berkley Publishing Group,
a division of Penguin Group (USA) Inc.,
375 Hudson Street, New York, New York 10014.

ISBN: 978-0-425-23313-9

BERKLEY® PRIME CRIME
Berkley Prime Crime Books are published by The Berkley Publishing Group,
a division of Penguin Group (USA) Inc.,
375 Hudson Street, New York, New York 10014.
BERKLEY® PRIME CRIME and the PRIME CRIME logo are trademarks of Penguin Group (USA)
Inc.

PRINTED IN THE UNITED STATES OF AMERICA

10 9 8 7 6 5 4 3 2 1

If you purchased this book without a cover, you should be aware that this book is stolen property. It was reported as "unsold and destroyed" to the publisher, and neither the author nor the publisher has received any payment for this "stripped book."

This book is dedicated with eternal devotion to the boy who sat beside me in seventh grade and generally annoyed the heck out of me. The blind date I discovered I knew, the man I married, and the father of my children. My best friend, and my heart's haven. Bob Blair, who makes every book possible, and taught me that love means never having to clean the snow off my own car.

Author's Note

Mystick Falls and its police department are figments of my imagination situated near the delightfully real Mystic, Connecticut, where Madeira Cutler's fictional vintage clothing shop is located. Also real are: the World War II spy mentioned later in the book, Ferncliff Cemetery and the stars interred there, and Coco Chanel's little black dress, as described, though it may not still exist today. *Diamond Sands*, the off-Broadway musical, is also a figment of my imagination.

One

Women dress alike all over the world: they dress to be annoying to other women.　　　　　　　—ELSA SCHIAPARELLI

As I drove to work that morning, I remembered the dream I'd had last night: Me as a toddler being passed between my mother and Aunt Fiona, the two of them dancing and chanting in rhyme beside the Mystic River beneath a full and magical moon.

Not a new dream, but an omen. Something in my life was about to change, *possibly* for the better.

I bit my lip, until from the top of the hill I saw the gorgeous weather vane atop my building, a ship with a mellow copper-green patina, sailing in the wind in whatever direction the universe determined.

The sight never failed to add to my sense of destiny.

No wonder I always arrived jazzed. After all, wearing designer vintage fashions is practically a requirement for a vintage dress shop owner. Every delightful day.

I mean, how lucky can a girl get? I was home again. No more designing clothes for Faline in New York City. Faline, who took credit for everyone's designs. She who must be loved and obeyed and agreed with, ad nauseum.

But that was the past. Today, I was looking toward the future.

In deference to my dream, feeling the need to be ready for anything, I'd chosen an eighties Jean Muir "perfect suit" with a flare at the waist and a red that brought ripe raspberries to mind. Given the snow, I wore sturdy boots and carried my fifties Ferragamos with spool heels and gloved-suede arches in the same red.

To add whimsy to classic perfection, I picked a Lulu Guinness "mansion" bag that looked like a handbag shop with a black-and-white-striped awning and a scattering of red and pink purses in the windows.

As I turned from Main to Bank Street, the architectural beauty and eye-pleasing colors of my shop—sage, eggplant, and lavender—filled me with joy.

I revel in every assurance that my restoration of the former morgue–cum–funeral chapel carriage house adds a certain cachet to the charm of historic downtown Mystic.

I believe it and I wallow in it. I attempt to endow the luxurious enchantment of that confidence into the original fashions I design under my own Mad Magic label.

You see, I'm a recent escapee from the highest levels of the New York fashion industry. You can call me Mad, or Maddie, unless you're my father, Professor Harry Cutler, in which case you will call me Madeira, whether I want you to or not.

As for the magic halves of my shop and label, I'm also my mother's daughter, not a witch, precisely, but I have this whole psychic thing going on, which I apparently inherited from her. I can't ask her to confirm Aunt Fiona's assertion. Mom died when I was ten, though she still watches out for me, especially since I came back to Connecticut. Mom was a first-class chocoholic, so the sudden scent of chocolate, with no one in sight, is a—you'll excuse the pun—dead giveaway.

Compared to Mom, I'm merely fudging my way up the sweet-tooth ranks. Besides chocolate, I'm into seeking and selling delectable retro fashions and spreading the joy of the classic lines.

My life seems perfect, doesn't it, but there's one drawback: Certain vintage clothes speak to me, in more ways than the norm and often about dead people. I not only "hear" what they have to say, the outfits I touch give me visions, during which I often zone out to view and hear snippets of greed, jealousy, hate, vengeance, secrets, all of which often translate into: means, motive, and opportunity, vintage style.

But since everything's been quiet on the psychometric front for several months now, I'm hoping that was only a phase.

I pulled into my plowed parking lot rimmed in mounded snow, where a Wings Special Delivery truck sat beside my best friend Eve's Mini Cooper. Eve, aka the dress-in-black-to-please-myself man magnet, had already taken to charming the driver's khaki winter socks off.

"Hey," I said, joining them. "Am I late?"

"No, I'm early as usual," Eve said, "and glad of it."

I had in one hand a clear glass vase overflowing with red and white carnations as she filled the other with a mint mocha chip Frappuccino topped with chocolate whipped cream, my newest vice, while she shoved the morning paper between my purse straps and my arm.

With her hands now free, she signed for and accepted the box from the driver before she slipped her business card into Tall, Tan, and Do Me's pocket. "Later," she told him with a wink.

I don't know if he winked back. The fur trim at the top front of his leather aviator hat—earflaps down—tilted a bit too far forward, and his jacket's knit turtleneck stood zipped straight up to his goggles, presumably to protect him from snow glare . . . at thirty thousand feet, maybe.

Eve and I watched until his truck turned east on Main and disappeared, and I realized that I'd never heard his voice. "You're my hero," I said, eyeing Eve's overall getup. "So, Boobs McCleavage, is that a corset top pushing your assets up and out there? Are you going psychic on me? You're dressed like you *knew* a new hunk was coming into your life."

"Nah, it's part of my new look. Do you like it?"

"I love it. It's so *not* you."

"Gee, thanks, she who stuffs her A cup."

I chuckled. "A and a half," I said correcting her. "Did the guy join your stud-of–the-month club or what?"

Eve shivered, winked, and zipped up her black military jacket to protect her slightly ruffled, goose-pimply cleavage from the snow-swirling elements. "He will."

Two

After breathing, eating and sleeping—and excluding a couple of delicious optional extras—one of the fundamental pleasures of the human body is to clothe it.
  —LINDA WATSON, *TWENTIETH CENTURY FASHION*

❧

I took Chakra, my guard kitty, from between my Honda Element's two front seats, where her new cat carrier fit perfectly. I'd designed it for winter or summer. Right now, it was double snuggly with its removable sherpa lambs' wool cashmere lining—printed with black paws on taupe. An adapter for the also-removable warming pad beneath her plugged into my dashboard.

"Boy, Chakra rides in style," Eve said. "You gonna sell those carriers in your shop?"

"Maybe," I said, "though they might be a bit too modern for a vintage dress shop."

"Yeah, the moonroof's a dead giveaway."

"Hey," I said. "For summer, it has a zip-on Florida room. Highly sought after."

"What, no pool?"

I elbowed Eve as I unlocked my shop's lavender door and the bells in my wreath made of handmade purple and magenta hearts—no two alike—tinkled.

Inside, Dante Underhill, former undertaker and hunky housebound ghost, waited for our usual morning chat. He even saluted when Chakra, at the sight of his ghostly self, banshee-howled "Ma-dei-ra," as always, at the top of her overdeveloped kitty lungs, her version of my name never failing to make Dante smile and shake his head. I opened Chakra's carrier so she could begin her morning rounds.

Dante had seventy years' worth of juicy gossip to share and tended to serve it to me in detailed, breakfast-sized portions that set me up for the day.

I had never enjoyed gossip more, mostly because I knew some of the aging players, or at least I'd heard of them from their descendents. Mild-mannered neighbors, or their ancestors, with checkered pasts. Who'd a thunk it?

Today, however, Dante saw Eve, saluted, and disappeared. Eve didn't often join me at the shop mornings, because she taught computer science at UConn, but when she came, she stuck around for a while.

Eve didn't know Dante existed, and since she got a bit edgy where ghosts and magic were concerned, I'd never mentioned my ghostly Cary Grant clone.

None the wiser, she relaxed in what I thought of as Dante's chair to read the morning paper, and before long, after I'd traded my boots for my Ferragamos and hung my coat, Chakra curled up on Eve's lap.

First order of business, find a vintage purse in unsaleable condition to decorate my counter. Today it was a Badgley Mischka crocodile in jungle red into which I set my overflowing vase of red and white carnations and baby's breath. Gorgeous. A yummy conversation piece, vintage style.

Basically, I tortured myself every few days by breaking my heart over what people did to classic vintage purses but I consoled myself by using them as Vintage Magic bouquet holders.

Chakra jumped to the counter to sniff, circle, and generally check it out before she meowed her approval, hopped to the floor, and strolled over to catapult into Eve's embrace.

After I turned the sign to Open, I took a pair of scissors to the package delivered by a man dressed like a flying squirrel.

Leery about touching a potential vintage clothing item I knew nothing about, because of my visions and the unsolved murders they'd dragged me into, I carefully parted tissue layers, touching only the paper.

I recognized the dress immediately but could hardly wrap my brain around having it in my shop. About ten years ago, while in fashion school, I won the opportunity to design this awesome seafoam gown, trimmed in pricey cubic zirconias, for a Broadway actress, now a dear friend. But since she, too, collected designer vintage and one-of-a-kind originals, I couldn't imagine why she would have sent a dress we both loved back to me.

Dominique DeLong had always been a die-hard note writer and wouldn't send an email if her life depended on it. So I fished through the tissue, careful not to touch the dress, and finally found the familiar embossed parchment envelope that could not have slipped to the bottom of the box, since it was taped—aka hidden?—between layers and layers of tissue.

Keeping my itchy fingers away from the dress in the box, I opened the envelope carefully and tried to shrug off the shivering heebie-jeebies raising the hair along my nape and arms.

Mad, sweetie, Dominique had written. *I always wanted you to have this. I hoped someday to give it to you, in person. If you have it, and not from my hand, I'm dead.*

I wanted to get it to you before it was too late. At any rate, "Tag. You're it. Run, do not walk, to the nearest exit."

Use your talents wisely. Love, Dom.

Three

Design is a revelation to me. It's like taking something that is
not alive and giving it form, shape, substance, and life.

—GEOFFREY BEENE

"Is this some kind of sick joke?" I snapped, denial beat-
ing in my chest. "Dominique DeLong is dead?"

"I'll say." Eve sat forward, waking Chakra so the kitten stretched and teased the newspaper into playing with
her. "It's all over the *Times*," Eve said, holding the paper
from Chakra's reach. "It says here that the actress collapsed during an off-Broadway musical performance of
Diamond Sands."

"I don't believe you." I'd tried to speak emphatically,
but my words trailed off in a telltale whisper.

Denial. Worry. Despair.

The sound of Chakra pouncing on the newspaper like
a baby kangaroo as Eve turned the headlines my way
woke me to the truth and tore at my subconscious denial,

until I focused on the visual: The headlines proclaiming her death and the picture of Dom at her most glamorous broke me.

For once the newspapers weren't touting Dominique DeLong's downward-spiraling career. The fact that they printed such a great picture told the story. The first rule of journalism: The skank cat you clawed yesterday is today's Saint Feline, if she's dead.

Dominique DeLong was indeed . . . gone.

I bit my lip, willed my tight chest to ease and my rising tears to recede. My trembling legs made it necessary for me to lower myself to my tapestried fainting couch. "Dom would rather have died *on* Broadway than off," I said, more to myself than Eve, aware I was in shock.

"At least there were witnesses," Eve said. "Hundreds of them, according to the papers."

My stomach flipped, and while I hadn't been aware that I shivered, Dominique's note trembled in my hand. "Witnesses?" Until that moment, I hadn't acknowledged the need, but the word in print surely implied suspicion and the need for witnesses.

On the other hand, it was a damned crying crime that Dom passed away in her forties with scads of untapped talent and star potential gone to waste.

No real crime had been categorically stated. It was the embryonic sleuth in me that grasped suspicion and looked for someone to blame. Wasn't it?

Chakra sensed my panic, jumped ship, left Eve, and leapt into my lap, curling against me. My kitten had the ability to physically soothe the angst in my solar plexus chakra—hence her name.

It wasn't long before her uncanny ability to ease the clutch in my gut had the desired effect. Not that my sorrow dissipated, but my intention to live reestablished itself.

I sighed and ran my hand down my baby cat's soft fur. "Chakra's grown less yellow with age. Have you noticed?" I asked Eve, who looked back at me with silent understanding and soul-mate commiseration.

"She's more cream now with this hint of a gold-tan in her forming stripes." Eve's interest said she understood that concentrating on Chakra soothed me like nothing else could. Well, Nick could, in his own way, but he was another story.

Eve looked down at her paper and continued reading, then she gasped and sat forward. "You know the infamous diamonds that Dominique wore around her eyes like a super bling eye mask during the finale of each show?"

"The ones she wore while she sang 'Diamonds Are a Girl's Best Friend'?" I confirmed. "The priceless gems loaned to the production by its sponsor, Pierpont Diamonds, as a publicity stunt?" I asked, trying to follow the weird change of topic.

"Right. They disappeared sometime between Dominique's death and her arrival at the hospital. She was DOA."

That fast, I pulled my hands from the vicinity of the

dress box, because this was no time to slip and touch its potentially brain-frying contents. A dress with a potential story to tell.

Diamonds, a good motive for . . . No, I wouldn't speak it, because saying the word "murder" made it more likely to be true.

Why the note? Why to me? "When did she die?" I asked.

Eve looked up from the paper. "She collapsed during one of those late night performances they have off-Broadway, the ten o'clock show. There seems to be a time issue that isn't clear, here, but time of death is *estimated* at approximately midnight."

I lost my breath and my heart pounded as if chasing after it. Winded for no reason, I looked at the dress box, reread the note that Dom implied she hadn't mailed, and I considered the unrealistically short span between her estimated time of death in New York City and the arrival of the Wings delivery truck in Mystic, Connecticut.

Dominique's note swam before my eyes.

Could someone have overnighted it *before* she died? Someone who *knew* she *would* die that night?

We'd had dinner together in New York a few weeks ago. She shared some dirt about her ex-husband, a member of the hangers-on, the entourage she bitingly called "the Parasites."

I'd told her that night, in strictest confidence, about my weird ability to read certain vintage clothing items, angling for a sleepover and a chance to read the original Chanel dress that once belonged to Coco herself.

Don't judge me. Who wouldn't want a glimpse into that world? Though there was no guarantee I'd see a thing.

Rather than show the excitement I expected, she'd given a half nod and said maybe I'd get a chance one of these days—not *we'd* get a chance. Then she asked if I wanted dessert and suggested cheesecake, "cholesterol be damned," she said like someone had taken control over the type-A, size-four health nut.

Again, I read her note, those final words echoing in her world-class smoky voice. "Use your talents wisely."

My talents.

Wooly knobby knits. She so did *not* mean dress design.

Four

Americans have an abiding belief in their ability to control reality by purely material means . . . airline insurance replaces the fear of death with the comforting prospect of cash.

—CECIL BEATON

Eve's brows furrowed. "Hey, how did *you* know Dominique was dead when I was the one reading the newspaper?"

I handed Eve Dom's note, wondering who could have sent the dress and how Dom could have anticipated their move?

Unless the box was already packed and addressed to me.

But why would it be, if Dominique wanted to hand me the dress herself? Though she and her money did have a huge and magnificent ability to *motivate* the Parasites, which may be how Dom knew I'd get the dress one way or another.

I knew Kyle, Dom's son, who she did not consider a

member of the Parasites, and he pretty much distrusted all of them, including his father.

I was mostly a trusting person, and Dom's opinion of them could have influenced mine, but if the rest were like Ian DeLong, Dom's ex and Kyle's father, her description of the Parasites were correct, the lot of them were like stick-figure piggy banks with neon signs on their Botoxed foreheads that flashed "feed me" whenever they looked Dom's way.

Money, always a good motive for . . . anything shady.

Still I could not believe that Dominique DeLong had been murdered.

Nevertheless, I took the Wings packaging from the trash, in the event cause of death turned out to be suspicious, in which case, a handwriting analysis of the label might be in order.

I was thinking more like a sleuth every day. Nick, my FBI boy toy would be proud. My nemesis, Mystick Falls's Detective Sergeant Lytton Werner would be horrified.

When Eve finished reading Dom's note, more than once, apparently, her head came up, her face a mask of confusion. "Huh?"

"Exactly."

"Did you tell Dominique that you could read vintage clothes?"

"Afraid so, a few weeks ago, but she promised me she'd take the knowledge to the grave."

Eve's eyes widened. "Mad, wake up and smell the crazy."

I caught Eve's panic but I refused to buy into it. "Oh, for the love of Gucci, you're talking coincidence, here."

"I'm not talking anything. You're reading my mind or you're thinking the same thing I am. Take it to her grave? Talk about a quick turnaround."

"There's only one way to prove you wrong," I said.

"What?" Eve asked, suddenly wary. "You're not going to try on the gown to find out what it knows?" Eve shot to her feet, combat boots prepared for flight. "Because if you are, I'm outta here."

"You don't get it, Goth Girl."

She calmed and unzipped her jacket. "Notice the ruffles? I'm trying to go for the steampunk look, thank you very much."

I slapped a hand to my heart. "I could get into dressing you in steampunk. But you need to dress less like a fighter pilot and more like a Victorian lady. Steampunk's not conservative. The corset's a good start but I'm talking frills, lace, leather, metal, gears."

"All black," Eve said.

"Of course, black, except for the metallic colors." I sighed. Eve didn't know it, but if I ever got married, I planned to make my bridesmaids wear red. A true test of friendship for my black-wearing brainiac BFF with a stubborn streak. My internal smile did me good, under the sad, creepazoid circumstances.

"So if reading Dominique's dress is not what you

planned," Eve said bringing me back to the present with a jolt, "what are you going to do to find out what happened to her?"

"Snoop. We're going to snoop."

"We? Where exactly is *my* name written on your insanity plea?"

Five

Fashion is like the ashes left behind by the uniquely shaped flames of the fire, the trace alone revealing that a fire actually took place.
　　　　　　　　　　　　　　　　　　—PAUL DE MAN

❧

I'd scared Eve more than once when working on a vintage outfit in her presence, because when there was a message to be seen, I often zoned out to read it. With a particularly informative piece of vintage clothing, I could go a bit zombie-like.

Evidently, I could also speak . . . in someone else's voice.

One of those times, watching and hearing me, Eve had nearly passed out. Eve, the strong.

Snooping sometimes got a bit dicey, too. Like when we confronted a killer and Eve had to knock him out to get his hands from around my throat.

Yes, I understood her reluctance, but I wasn't going to let her get away with it. "Put on your big-girl knickers, Meyers," I said. "No need to go all girly-girl and faint. The first thing I'm going to do with Dom's dress is take it to the climate-controlled safe room in Nick's basement."

"Whew!" Eve wiped her brow for show as she sat down again. But she furrowed the same as she crossed her legs. "Why take it to Nick's? Why not to your house?"

"Because Nick's new house came with a panic room that I'm using as a temporary cold storage unit until I can afford to have part of my upstairs storage room, here, turned into one. And because my father's house is old, damp, and some of our ghostly residents have a habit of leaving doors open."

"Guess they didn't have climate control in George Washington's day," Eve said, speaking of my father's house, an old tavern moved from the older Boston Post Road. It had the documented distinction of once hosting the father of our country, and Thomas Jefferson, as well, at different times, of course.

Eve checked the spikes in her badass black hair to make sure they'd still draw blood. "I would have bet that not a single house in Mystick Falls had a safe room," she said.

"Well, *one* does, a pricey unit at that, as primo as the house. My vintage furs are already there."

"I suppose that half *your* clothes are also at Nick's new place." Eve raised a winged brow, her full mahogany-glossed mouth pursed in disapproval.

"You don't want to make that bet, Meyers." I often juggled the grudging relationship between my on-again/off-again studly Italian FBI agent, Nick Jaconetti, and Eve, who'd been my best friend since kindergarten. Nick and I only went back to junior high. High school really.

"Can you keep an eye on the shop while I go lock this up?" I asked, changing back into my snow boots, then slipping into my black Sonia Rykiel coat with capelet collar. I slid the box with Dominique's gown into a canvas bag that advertised Vintage Magic with a tasteful arrangement of primo pumps and purses.

Eve checked her watch. "Sure, I'm not teaching a class today."

With the gown burning a stress ulcer in my gut like the lit end of one of Coco Chanel's own ciggy butts, I made it halfway to the door before Detective Sergeant Lytton Werner walked in. "Miss Cutler, Miss Meyers," he said, tipping his nonexistent hat.

This was not the man that Eve and I got drunk with on Dos Equis with Mexican takeout some months ago. Lytton Werner had crawled so far back into his hard outer shell—as far as we were concerned—he was likely to crack his tailbone bending over backward to be polite.

Chakra deserted Eve to pounce into Werner's arms and give him a little head-rubbing snuggle against his neck.

I could tell that Werner was as delighted as surprised by the show of trust and affection from Traitor Cat. "Hey there, little one," he said, giving Chakra his full attention, which, of course, made it so much easier for him to ignore me and Eve.

Lytton Werner—I'll always be sorry that I called him Little Wiener when we were in third grade—shouted it, actually, in a cafeteria full of students. Frankly, I didn't know *what* I was calling the bully. A naming-rhyme payback had been my simple intent. What third grader knows she's maligning someone's manhood before he's reached it?

Who knew the name "Little Wiener" would stick like frickin' forever, a glue bonding and solidifying the animosity between us . . . except when we stepped into the shadowlands of heightened awareness during our infrequent investigations.

Werner cleared his throat as if he could see inside my brain while I shivered and pulled myself from the limb-prickling trance brought on by our locked gazes.

Eve, too, cleared her throat, but her, I could ignore.

"To what do we owe the pleasure, Detective?" I asked, my voice an octave too high.

Werner's eyebrow twitched as if he matched my fake pleasure and raised it. He cleared his throat. "An abandoned Wings truck was found in the nearest Wings warehouse parking lot a short time ago," he said.

My heart began to race but I hoped I hid it well. "And that's of interest to me, because?"

"It's registered in New York. It's empty. Key in the ignition. Wiped suspiciously clean of fingerprints. No cargo. Nothing inside, except this." He handed me a piece of paper.

"Oh," I said. "An internet map starting in New York City and heading straight to my shop." A map. A tucking map leading Werner here.

Werner rocked on his heels. "We found a miniscule corner of that map sticking up from beneath the floor mat beneath which it was hidden. Your name and the name of your shop are written, as you see, Unabomber-style, at the top."

I shrugged as if I couldn't care less. "We did get a seven A.M. delivery from Wings." There was no need to share my concerns with him. Even if Dominique's death turned out to be suspicious—which to me it already was—the nefarious deed took place in New York City and not in Lytton's jurisdiction: Mystic and Mystick Falls, Connecticut.

"Damn," Eve said. "I guess my date with that driver is off."

Werner's accusatory gaze snapped from me to Eve. "You saw the driver?"

Eve and I both nodded.

Lytton put Chakra on the counter as he pulled his notebook from the pocket of his tan detective-style trench coat, his investigative antennae quivering. "Hair color?" he asked.

Eve stood. "Er."

"Um." I described his facial cover-up. "So we didn't see his hair."

Werner growled deep in his chest.

Unfortunately, Eve was able to describe the rest of

the courier's body in unnecessary detail, "squeezable tush and sculpted lips" included.

"Any identifying marks?"

"He wore gloves," Eve said.

I snapped my fingers. "Emporio Armani, logo labeled. Men's dark brown, napa leather."

Six

Design must seduce, shape, and perhaps more importantly,
evoke an emotional response.   —APRIL GREIMAN

❧

Eve and Lytton stared at me like I had two heads, neither
a designer original.

"So I know clothes and designers," I said in self-
defense. "So shoot me, but we can trace those gloves
back to the retailer."

Eve turned to Werner. "Maddie just made me remember something. The guy had a dragonfly tat at the edge
of the glove on his right lower arm. I wouldn't have seen
it if I hadn't nearly dragged the glove off, trying to pull
him closer."

"Why so interested in an abandoned truck?" I asked
Werner.

"APB." Werner replied without looking up from his

note taking. "It was stolen last night around midnight in New York City."

Oops.

His head came up as he examined my expression. Did he hear me cringe inwardly? "The ambulance that took that movie star to the hospital had also been stolen."

My heart skipped a beat, but I didn't let it show. "Lots of vehicles are stolen every night in New York City, Detective. What's the connection?"

"There isn't one that the FBI can find."

"The Feds are in on this?"

"Stolen diamonds are known to fund terrorist activities, so yes, there's an FBI investigation. Not to mention that Pierce Pierpont, current scion and head of the Pierpont Diamond Mines, has political clout, and he, of course, wants his diamonds found.

"But a stolen ambulance that carried a famous movie actress, who died under mysterious circumstances, is certainly cause for speculation."

Mysterious circumstances. Baste it, I knew it.

"Also, the lengthy time lapse between the ambulance's departure from the theater and the time it was found bearing Dominique DeLong's body, siren blasting, at the hospital's emergency room entrance, missing its driver, allowed for more than enough time for a diamond robbery to take place."

"You mean they ripped the diamonds off her face while she was unconscious? Poor Dom. That must have been so painful."

"No," Werner said. "All indications are that she died instantly and on stage. They took the diamonds after she died."

My stomach flipped while my brain fired like popcorn, my thought processes having multiple partings of the way. Should I admit that I knew Dominique, that I was carrying a dress that might—if one had a wild imagination—be construed as evidence? Or should I let it ride until I talked to Nick?

Dom's death touched me, rocked my world, and the diamonds were only an afterthought. "All this because somebody misplaced a few diamonds in New York City? They're probably still in the woman's dressing room." It wasn't easy to distance myself from Dom at this point, but for Werner's sake, I felt it necessary for the moment. Dom hadn't exactly been a neat freak, not even when it came to her pricey baubles. She liked to make the Parasites earn their keep and pick up after her.

I shook my head. "They should be looking into what happened to Dominique, not the diamonds."

"The NYPD are also looking into what happened to Ms. DeLong," Werner said. "Never fear."

"Good." Still trying to decide whether to out the dress, evidence wise, I decided to pay attention to a family echo in the voices of my siblings, who coined the phrase: *"Shut up, Mad!"*

Decision made. "If we've answered your questions, Detective, I have an errand to run."

Werner nodded toward my newly delivered package. "Is that the box Wings brought?"

Scrap! From the corner of my eye, I saw Eve slip the note from Dominique into her folded newspaper, so I relaxed and handed Werner the box.

He opened it, folded back the tissue, and whistled. "This is primo designer, isn't it? From Paris maybe? Mucho bucks?"

"Thank you, Detective."

"Why thank me?"

"I designed it."

That surprised him. If I didn't know better, I'd think respect laced his regard, until he frowned and looked more closely at me. "Why are your eyes red?"

I hated that Werner noticed small personal details about me. I raised my chin. "Someone I care about passed away."

"I'm sorry to hear that." He took the canvas bag from my limp hand, slid the empty packaging out, saw the return address, and whistled. "That dead movie star? You knew *her*?" A baited accusation if ever I'd heard one.

I gritted my teeth, a bad and costly habit. "She was a Broadway star, not a movie star. Dominique, yes, that's her. Please have some respect and stop tossing about the word 'dead' as if it were a color."

"My apologies and condolences," Werner said, and he meant it, "but that dress could be evidence."

"It's a gift. I made it for her, and she left it to me. Period."

"Too bad somebody felt the need to steal a truck to get it to you."

Double scrap with a "tucking A" thrown in for trim. My ringing cell phone saved me from responding. I'd never been so grateful for the opportunity to answer it.

My caller's voice shocked the Hermès out of me. "Kyle! I'm so sorry about your mom."

Werner mouthed "speakerphone," so I had no choice but to set my phone down so we could all hear what Kyle had to say. Well, I might have argued, because this had nothing to do with Werner, but I would only look as guilty as I felt if I refused the request.

"It's sad and chaotic here," Kyle said, "but Mom left strict instructions about what she wanted done after she died."

"Funeral arrangements, you mean?"

"They're not releasing the b—*her*—until the investigation is finished. Uh, no, not instructions for her funeral. I haven't been able to bring myself to read those instructions yet."

I was confused. "But she left instructions for after she died? When did she take the time to do that?"

"They're dated two weeks ago. Weird, I know."

So had Dom been suicidal? Suspicious? What?

Kyle cleared his throat, the sound of a man who's trying to deny emotion. "These instructions have to do with her vintage clothes," Dom's son said. "She wants— wanted—the collection to raise money for charity during a big fashion show produced while she's still in the

29

news and that you should arrange the show. She left a list of causes for you to split the proceeds among, but she suggested that you hold the show there in Mystic to pull in collectors from Newport, Rhode Island, Boston, and New York City. You can invite anyone you want. Can I count on you, Aunt Mad?"

Oh, great, play the aunt card in front of Werner. Okay, so Kyle had been twelve when I was nineteen, but time should have erased our age difference, and it would have, if he wasn't asking for a favor. A big favor.

"Of course, Kyle." But I'd sure like to see Dominique's instructions, I thought.

"Good. Thanks. After the fashion show, I have permission to sell her collection at a private auction, if I want to, and I'm not sure that I do. Mom included a list of the people she wanted you to invite to both events, but you get first pick of the vintage clothes you want before you host an auction, if there is one."

"I'm overwhelmed." No fooling.

"Anyway, I'm allowed to sell them all except for a dress she wanted you to have, and don't worry, Aunt Mad, I'm sure I'll find it, eventually."

Werner glanced at the dress box delivered that morning, as did I, then we glanced at each other.

I shrugged. Could be a different dress, right?

"Kyle, it sounds as though your mother knew she was going to die."

The phone went dead.

Seven

The energy of imagination, deliberation, and invention, which fall into a natural rhythm totally one's own, maintained by innate discipline and a keen sense of pleasure—these are the ingredients of style. And all who have it share one thing: originality.   —DIANA VREELAND

I'd say one thing for Dominique, given her elaborate after-death plans. She was an original.

The sudden silence of the phone going dead left us stunned and staring at the silent thing as the first customer of the day arrived. A redhead. A gorgeous redhead, as bundled up and unidentifiable as the Wings delivery man.

She held her head upright and walked like a runway model. Female perfection, she displayed, in an all-encompassing red Valentino cape, a colorful Hermè's scarf that seemed to celebrate warm colors, and a pair of eighties Manolo boots, white with red heels. And she carried a retro white bunny muff.

The Lady in Red looked out of place at this end of Connecticut, even in a shop as upscale as mine.

Wandering my fashion nooks, aimlessly, from Mad as a Hatter to Little Black Dress Lane, she threw an occasional glance our way, peeking *over* her rose-colored glasses.

Not prescription, then, and were they an intentional metaphor?

When I looked back at Werner, I set the tips of my fingers beneath his chin to raise his jaw. "You got a little drool on your chin."

He firmed his lips and stuck his hands in the pockets of his Mickey Spillane trench coat. "Listen," he said, purposely turning his back on the Lady in Red. "You'd tell me if you were in trouble, right, Mad?"

Now he was using my nickname? Lytton was letting honest concern dislocate his polite, if feigned, indifference.

"I've lost a good friend," I said, "but I'm not in trouble." That I know of. Yet.

My cell phone rang, again. And, again, it was Kyle, so I grabbed the bag with the boxed dress in it, walked to the dressing rooms, where Eve and Werner followed, and I set my cell phone down so we could listen while my customer could not.

I, however, stood in the doorway to keep an eye on both the shop and the Lady in Red.

"Sorry, Aunt Mad, for cutting you off like that."

"What happened?" I asked.

"People are calling and knocking at the door. Some of them brought maids carrying casseroles, but I told

Higgins to send them away. I'm not receiving guests until seven tonight.

"Higgins said they're coming to offer their condolences, but they seem more like vultures who want to pick at the gristle surrounding Mom's death. Frankly, the whole thing's freaking me out."

"What can I do to help?" I asked.

"I don't suppose you feel like coming to stay for a couple of days, like before seven tonight? I can't wade through this catty Broadway love/hate gossip suck, alone, and I can't trust any of Mom's . . . whatever they are."

Parasites, I thought. "Why can't you?"

"I should think that would be obvious, but that's like the last thing she told me. Don't trust the—well—the people who've leeched her dry. Damn, Dad's here. I can hear his voice. Higgins likes him. He's gonna let the jerk in, I know it."

Now, that's bad, I thought. Greedy, bitter Ian De-Long, Dominique's philandering ex-husband, is the biggest scavenger of them all. His favorite form of self-flattery was a line I could hit him for. In referring to Dom's celebrity status, he would say, "She wouldn't be a DeLong, if it wasn't for me."

As if his name had *anything* to do with her success.

As her business partner, Ian owned half of Dominique, a circumstance that not even a dirty divorce had been able to erase. And it was entirely possible that he was about to inherit the other half of DeLong Ltd. jewelry, perfume, and accessory design interests, not to mention Dom's highly popular tell-all books turned movies.

"Can you wait in the den, Dad?" Kyle swore beneath his breath. "You're the executor, did you know?"

I straightened and took my gaze from the shop. "What? Kyle, who were you talking to just now?"

"You. You're the executor. Of Mom's will. You, Aunt Mad. You knew, right?"

Son of a slip stitch. "No, I did not know."

Kyle made a tsking sound. "You should see the instructions she left for you on that score. And I'm talking musical score here."

I pinched the top of my nose to stop my throbbing brain swell. Dominique hadn't been kidding when she said, "Tag, you're it." I sighed. I needed to go. I wanted to go. For Dom. For her son. "Give me a few hours to get the shop in order. I'll try to be there by seven, but I can't guarantee I'll make it." I looked at my watch. "Well, nearly ten hours. Maybe."

"Call me when you're on your way. I'll send a car. And thanks, Aunt—"

"Kyle. Drop the 'aunt.' Call me Mad. You've caught up with me. We're both the same age now."

His chuckle eased the ache in my chest, for both our sakes.

Everything would be okay, I told myself, though it wouldn't, really. Dead was dead. His mother. My friend.

Dead . . . forever.

Eight

"Style" is an expression of individualism mixed with cha-
risma. Fashion is something that comes after style.

—JOHN FAIRCHILD

I snapped my phone shut, slipped it in my suit pocket,
and turned to Werner. "As you heard, I'll be going to
New York. I just have to see if Aunt Fiona is available to
run the shop."

"Good thing she went into semiretirement," Eve
said.

I shrugged. "Sometimes I think she did that for me, to
help me with the shop."

Eve tilted her head. "I think she did it for your
father."

I chuckled. "Detective, thank you for your patience
and understanding this morning."

He tipped his nonexistent hat, left the dressing room,
and went to the door, without so much as a glance to-

ward my unusual customer in red, but he did stop and turn back to me. "Stay out of trouble, will you?"

"I resent that."

He shrugged. "I mean, be safe."

"You sweet-talker, you."

He blushed but not for long. "I *actually* mean, don't look in people's windows, break into their houses, riffle through their things, steal their dogs, or tick off the NYPD."

I saluted. "You *will* tell me if you learn anything about that Wings truck, won't you?" I sort of begged.

"Since it appears to have been stolen to get to you, I will," he said, "if only for your own protection."

"I appreciate that."

The minute the door closed behind him, I turned to Eve. "Put Dom's note in my purse, will you?"

She immediately swiped it from the newspaper and did exactly that.

"Change of plans," I said. "Wait on our customer, will you? I'm going upstairs to call Nick."

"Is he on assignment?"

"Yes, but I'm going to try to lure him home with the promise of a diamond heist, New York style."

"What makes you think he'll leave the case he's already on?"

"I have my ways . . . with him."

"Barf," Eve said. "TMI."

I almost smiled as I climbed my enclosed stairway. In my nearly empty second floor: sewing nook in one corner, collection of caskets in another, and two, count them, two, horse-drawn hearses to the side, I had plenty of room to pace. Which I did while I waited for Nick to answer his cell phone. Sometimes when he was on assignment and he didn't want to be heard or noticed, he turned it off. This could be one of those times.

I was just about to give up when he answered. "Hey, ladybug," he said. "Sorry I took so long answering. I was in the shower."

"Good; if you've got a shower, you're probably not in a jungle somewhere."

"Great powers of deduction, but I'm home. I got in an hour ago."

"Is my brother, and your FBI partner, home, too?"

"Dropped Alex off myself."

"Good. I always do double duty in the worry department when you two are off on some top-secret assignment. Dad will be glad to hear it, too."

"I saw your father and Fiona strolling down your street as I drove by, so I stopped to say hello. Are those two an item?"

"Only in the minds of every Mystick Falls resident except them."

Nick chuckled.

"I'm glad Dad knows you and Alex are back. Did you see the morning papers?"

"I'm sorry about your friend, ladybug. Want to come over and be consoled?"

"Yes, but not now. Want to come to New York?"

"When?"

"Now? I got a package from Dominique this morning with a cryptic note that I'd love for you to see."

"I can read a note here."

"Dominique's son, Kyle, needs my help with the publicity hounds and gossipmongers chomping at the bits on his front steps. Besides, I'm the executor of Dom's will. Werner says that the FBI is working the missing Pierpont diamond case."

Silence.

I could hear the gears in Nick's brain start turning. "I've worked with the New York office before."

"I know. I was hoping you could connect, find out where things stand."

"Why?"

"Dom sort of asked me to."

"You only want me to go with you so you can use me."

I smiled. "So I promise not to use you."

His growl radiated meaning. "Wrong answer, but I'll change your mind. I'll pick you up in an hour."

Not if I get to you first, I thought.

Nine

Choose your corner, pick away at it carefully, intensely and to the best of your ability, and that way you might change the world.
—CHARLES EAMES

❧

Before I left, another odd customer showed, and Werner walked in behind him, as if the surly detective had been watching the place. He must have found the lip-glossed ski bum cause for concern.

The man had black-and-white-streaked hair artfully arranged to look messy and wore a designer ski outfit and goggles. I'm just surprised he wasn't carrying a pair of skis.

He did not come from Mystick Falls.

The pieces of his Mount Tom garb fit together too well, down to his slightly worn ski boots. Like the Lady in Red, who still graced the store, it seemed as if a theatrical costumer had dressed him.

That's what they looked like, theater people, both of them.

Worse, they walked around the shop as if they were stuck to opposing ends of magnets, like one couldn't get near the other because the pressure against it was too great.

In Dante's chair and from behind Eve's newspaper, Werner watched them as covertly as I did. Frankly, he looked like a retro, poverty-stricken cliché of a PI. The only thing missing was the cigarette dangling from his lips.

Werner aside, why would I have two such bizarro customers in one morning?

My day felt oddly orchestrated and transiently surreal, more so than the dream that started it. I picked up my bag with the boxed dress and packaging in it, glanced back at my weirdo customers, and gave Werner a helpless look.

He took off his coat. "Go," he whispered. "I'll put it down as a stakeout."

Eve released her breath and fell back in her chair. I hadn't realized that she'd been nervous about being left alone with the oddballs.

"I owe you," I told Werner, grabbing the canvas bag. "I'll take care of this and go find Aunt Fiona. I won't be long, I promise."

At Nick's house, I used my key to get in while looking forward to seeing him. A long separation could make for some hot fire, which we tended to shy away from. Nick and I have been toying with our sex-charged relationship, like kids and fire, since junior high.

We've both matured, but our relationship has remained somewhat static, unless you count the way in which we now express ourselves, with rare flashes of spontaneous combustion.

As soon as the fire gets too hot, however, we back away, both of us. We've never discussed it, but that's how we like it. I guess you could call it a semi-monogamous flirtation, no sparks barred, just infernos.

It also kept us safe from relationship shopping, blind dates, bad pickup lines, and poor choices. Gee, maybe we hadn't matured as much as I thought.

Go figure.

I left Dominique's gown in Nick's new living room, decorated with a heavy dollop of unpacked boxes. "Nick, where are you?"

"Up here."

I took the stairs at a fast clip. Hell, I hadn't seen him for more than a month. But when I found him . . . squeak!

My Italian stud turned from the sink in nothing but a pair of red silk boxers and one cheek's worth of shaving cream. One side of his mouth went up in a half smile, like he'd been caught with his pants down and liked my reaction.

Heart palpitations. Screw the fire.

I was in his arms before he could finish wiping his face, but that didn't matter to the kiss. He raised me, walked me to his bed, and we went down together.

The kiss, practiced and French, tasted like we were definitely on again, and it lasted long enough to catch up with our time apart. As clothes got unbuttoned, the heat in the room rose proportionally.

Spontaneous combustion was a near thing, and finishing what we shouldn't have started a dangerous possibility when time was not our friend.

I sat straight up and knocked Nick off the bed. "Friend! Dead. Can't," I said, falling back on my elbows, achingly aware of what I was about to miss. "New York. Now."

"So you came here, why?" he asked, getting up off the floor. "To help me get ready?" He frowned. "Ready for what?"

I bit my lip as I got up and rebuttoned my suit jacket. "Dom sent me a valuable gown, a collectable with great provenance. I need to lock it in your safe room before we go."

"I'd better go downstairs with you."

"Why? I know the way."

"My libido needs a time-out, preferably in cold storage."

"You'll freeze."

"If I'm lucky, though this doesn't *seem* to be my lucky day."

He slipped on a pair of tan casual slacks to accompany me downstairs and after that to walk me to the front door, but he didn't bother with a shirt, the tease. He knew how tempting I found his ripped muscles.

I gave him Dom's note to read, and after he did, he ran a hand through his hair, a dark tussled curl falling to his forehead as he whistled.

"I told you. Meet me at the shop when you finish packing. I have to see if Aunt Fee can run the shop for me while we're gone."

"I'm pretty sure she can."

"I've learned not to count on anything."

"Three days in New York together," he said as his mouth came for mine. "Three nights," he whispered, before he took the kiss slow and deep, and gave me a taste of the possibilities.

I sighed. "Man, you feel good."

He groaned deep in his chest and pushed me away. "For both our sakes."

Still, I hated the loss of his body heat. "Why am I supposed to go?" I asked, lust-dazed.

"Aunt Fee. Shop." He took me by the shoulders and turned me to face my car, then he half-patted, half-caressed my backside to prod me in the right direction.

His chuckle as I practically sleepwalked to my car reminded me of why he spoiled me for other men.

Ten

People should learn about their own styles and know more
about themselves.   —VIVIENNE TAM

I checked the mirror on my visor. Starry eyes, warm
pink cheeks, no lipstick left, my blush smudged with a
dollop of shaving cream.

Sex starved.

"Baste it, Mad, you've gotta get moving, here." I
looked back at the house and ogled temptation in the
flesh as Nick stood in the doorway, pulling one slow sus-
pender over his bare chest, a grin on his face.

I shook my fist at him.

He nodded and saluted as I backed down the drive.

Getting Aunt Fiona to work for me called for a face-to-
face, and if she and dad were still out walking together, I'd
catch two birds and all that. I could use a brisk walk myself
about now, to clear the cobwebs, and there were plenty.

I saw Dad and Aunt Fiona from two blocks away, arguing as usual, and they were loving every minute of it, as if the rest of the world didn't exist. That was new. Usually they wouldn't want anyone to hear them, which meant, arguing or not, they were wholly absorbed in each other.

The world as I knew it tilted on its axis.

My father had disliked Aunt Fiona the minute they met. She and my mother, best friends since college, had practiced witchcraft together, a belief system my father barely tolerated.

When my mother passed away, Dad and Aunt Fee had nothing more to say to each other that didn't involve us kids, especially me. Aunt Fiona had taught me the love of sewing, fashions, and all things handmade. Still, she and my dad barely spoke for nineteen years.

Then I came home to Mystick Falls to help my sister Sherry prepare for her wedding, never expecting her to become the prime suspect in a murder. I'd stayed to help and reconnected with Aunt Fiona, which fanned her and Dad's association and my love of vintage clothing.

Dad resisted, but last fall, when Aunt Fiona got locked in a casket—story for another day—Dad became her knight in shining armor, mostly because he mocked her, until he realized that the experience had scarred her.

Oh, Dad wouldn't acknowledge his knightly role, but he's there for her, even if it means that he sleeps on her sofa when she's freaked, or she sleeps in one of my siblings' old bedrooms, all empty except mine.

My sister Brandy's in the peace corps. Sherry lives nearby with her husband, Justin, which reminds me that I have a baby shower to plan for her. My brother, Alex, his wife Tricia, and toddler Kelsey, live near FBI headquarters in New Haven.

So if it wasn't for me living at Dad's, he and Aunt Fiona might get to be alone once in a while: my thought; probably not theirs. While this new "arrangement" between them has caused a great deal of over-the-fence chatter in Mystick Falls, the subjects of said gossip are oblivious.

Nevertheless, my father is laughing again, Fee's eyes are brighter, and, yes, they argue all the time, but with the enthusiasm of a debate club going for the gold.

When my dad isn't teaching English Lit at UConn, Aunt Fiona listens to him quote the literary greats.

A lawyer, Aunt Fee recently caused a gossip-ripe incident of her own when she went into semiretirement. Oddly, she works the same days dad teaches.

I'm telling you right now, if they say they're taking a trip to the Finger Lakes wine country, I'm putting my foot down. I do not need a baby sibling named Merlot.

They didn't hear me pull up behind them. They didn't hear me call their names. I ran to catch up, surprised them, fell into step beside them, and gave them a peek into "The Day That Weird Stood Still."

Less than an hour later, packed and ready to go, Nick was waiting for me at the shop, talking to Werner, while Dad and Aunt Fiona weren't far behind me.

"Nick," I said. "New aftershave? Yum."

"Emporio Armani Diamonds for men."

"Wow," I said. "Diamonds everywhere today."

"What does that mean?" Werner asked.

"Dominique collapsed performing *Diamond Sands* and singing 'Diamonds Are a Girl's Best Friend,' now her diamonds are missing, and here's Nick wearing the scent of diamonds. That's all I'm saying."

"Oh." Werner grabbed his coat.

I leaned into Nick's neck, closed my eyes, and inhaled. "Mmm, Bergamot, vetiver, and . . . cedar, I think." I opened my eyes, but my body was still on high alert. "A lethal combination."

"The better to please you with, my dear."

Eve made a gagging sound and Werner nodded as if he agreed. "Your dubious posers are gone," he said, speaking of the Lady in Red and ski boy, and snapping me back to my surroundings. "So I'll be on my way as well," Werner added. "Have a good trip."

"Thanks for staying," I said.

The frown lines on Werner's brow cleared. "Anytime."

The shop looked busy with normal tourists and locals. Yesterday, I had advertised my upcoming Valentine's Day intimate apparel sale and a special Men's Night, starting with hors d'oeuvres and manly thirst quenchers, previous to the arrival of several shapely friends who would model and describe the undies and peignoir sets, hopefully encouraging the men to purchase them as Valentine's Day gifts. This kind of event was big in New York, but here, I didn't know. I'd sent invites to upscale sports and country clubs to bring in the right buyers.

The sale is why most shoppers were clustered in the fashion nook called Corsets and Less, men and women alike checking out majorly sexy chemises and shirts in cotton from the Loire River valley, designer labels in silk crepe and Charmeuse, items by Cocoon, silk trimmed with hand-painted blossoms, and vintage P.J. Flannigan.

I mentally rubbed my hands together at the upswing in business. Things had been quiet since Christmas, and I hated like hell to leave after a successful ad, though today was only the first of the month.

"Don't worry," Aunt Fiona said, accurately reading me. "I can handle this."

"*We* can handle this," my dad said. "You'll only be gone a few days."

During this part of the trip, I thought. I hadn't told them about the fashion show to raise money for Dom's charities or the fact that I was executor of her will. I'd save those bombshells until I read her instructions.

"Your dad and I will work on the details for Men's Night," Aunt Fiona said. "Give you a head start."

"I'm coming to Men's Night," Nick said.

Eve rolled her eyes. "Perv. Let's go. I miss New York."

"*You're* not coming on this trip," Nick snapped.

"Maybe neither of us is." Eve laughed.

I elbowed her. "You don't even have a change of clothes."

"Sure I do." She indicated a rack of outfits. "I shopped for dial-down-the-ruffles steampunk. You made one huge sale while you were gone—to me. Fee, did you bring the travel bag?"

Aunt Fiona gave Nick a shrug and went out to her trunk for an empty suitcase.

"Let's get your bags in my trunk," my father told us while Eve finished packing her new wardrobe. "I'll take the three of you to the train station."

"Why are you coming with us, again?" Nick asked Eve.

"Mostly to be the burr beneath your saddle, boy toy. And I like New York."

Eleven

I love New York. But the energy is so intense.
—JOHN GALLIANO

❧

The train rolled into Penn Station around two o'clock, and as we walked toward the curb, Kyle DeLong stepped out of a metallic gold stretch Lamborghini limo. "Mad, I'm so grateful that you could come," he said, giving me an intense hug.

"This is some car," I said, trying to stop welling up at the thought of my reason for being here. "Was it your mother's?"

"No, this one belongs to Pierpont Diamond Mines. It's a loaner. Mom had a 1953 Bentley limo in two-tone silver. Not a stretch. I didn't have the heart to use it, not yet, anyway."

I was grateful as I introduced him to Eve, and though I started to introduce Nick, Eve and Kyle were as bedazzled as cartoon characters seeing each other for the first time. I half expected their eyes to pop out of their heads and meet in the middle. I could even hear a little cosmic "Boing!"

Finally, they awoke to the world around them and I was able to introduce Nick, who seemed amused by what we'd just witnessed.

For a young man grieving over the unexpected and suspicious loss of his mother, Kyle became the mature embodiment of a charming host, his instant clutch crush on Eve notwithstanding.

"Where were we?" Kyle asked. "Oh, Mom's vintage Bentley. That belongs to DeLong Limited, the parent company for her music, perfume, and accessories holdings."

Mega holdings. "Which you run, and well, your mother told me."

Kyle looked away for a minute, his throat muscles working, before he turned back to me. "I needed to know she believed that, Mad."

We got comfortable in facing seats as the silence began to stretch, for almost as long as the limo.

Nick cleared his throat. "I called FBI's New York field office," he told Kyle. "I have an appointment there in a few minutes to see what I can do to help with your mother's case. Do you mind dropping me off?"

"No problem. I appreciate your help," Kyle said. "But isn't it unusual for the police and the FBI to join forces in an investigation?" Kyle asked.

"Not at all, and it's happening more and more often, these days," Nick said. "Believe me. Especially in these high-profile cases."

"Higgins," Kyle told his driver. "First stop: Federal Plaza."

Remembering our phone call, I believed Higgins was also his butler.

"Nick, feel free to call Higgins when you're ready to be picked up. He'll give you his card with the number on it for when your meeting is over."

"Great. Thanks."

A half hour later, the Big Apple at its busiest, we watched Nick cross a bustling sidewalk and disappear into a skyscraper. Then Kyle asked Higgins to raise the privacy window.

"Okay," Kyle said leaning forward. "Pierpont Theater is closed to the public right now, but it won't be to us. I bought some insurance. Before I picked you up, I stopped by with a thank-you bottle of Scotch for the security guard. He was good to my mother. He should be out cold by now. A bit sneaky, but if it helps us find Mom's murderer, she won't mind."

"Do you know the cause of death yet?" I asked.

"Nobody is telling me anything," he said. "Neither the police nor the FBI are talking, at least not to me."

"Well, let's hope Nick brings some information back with him."

"Hey," Eve said. "What are you two up to? Are we actually breaking into the theater where Dom worked?"

"No," Kyle said. "We don't need to break in. The stage door will be open but the security guard will be asleep."

"And if somebody catches us?"

"I'm going back for my BlackBerry. One of the cops told me I could go in and get it, earlier today, but I didn't have time then, so I'm back for it now. I did that on purpose, too, so I could use it as an excuse when you got here. Nobody's due there for hours. Besides, I'm Dominique DeLong's son. I'm grieving for my mother. Maybe I just needed to sit in her dressing room for a while with my friends." His voice cracked on that one.

Eve's expression looked falsely stern and failed to hide the interest in her eyes over the prospect of breaking rules. "When did you two arrange this?" she asked us, suspicious.

"On the train, as soon as Nick made that appointment with the bureau, I called Kyle."

"You mean when you went to the ladies' room?"

"Yep." Pride laced my smile.

"I can't believe you're willingly stepping into another mystery. Not to mention the fact that Nick's not gonna like you sleuthing again."

"As I said, I can deal with Nick."

"Snort," Eve said to Kyle. "They've been apart for weeks. He'll be putty— No, no he won't. Yuckaflux! *Not* going *there*."

"Nick won't be a pushover if I get arrested," I added, "horny or not."

Higgins pulled the limo deep into the alley beside the Pierpont Theater and parked behind it. Kyle led us into the building from the side door as if he belonged there, which went a long way toward keeping me calm, as did the echoing snores of the security guard.

In the dark, where we entered the very old building, seating to the right, stage and dressing rooms to the left, it was easy to catch the scent of old theater, the sea of seats carrying a hint of must, musk, and cigar smoke, years' worth.

The closer we got to the stage, the stronger the scent of paint, makeup powder, nervous sweat. Dust and the scent of wood oil seemed to rise in waves from the stage floor.

Walking ahead of me, Eve hooked her arm through Kyle's, and he patted her hand as if he appreciated her support. Or he'd take care of her. Big surprise. All men wanted to take care of Eve, though my friend could sure take care of herself. Even younger men were attracted to her, it seemed. But hadn't I just told Kyle that the age difference between us had vanished. Little did I know that meant he'd fall for my best friend.

We walked as if through dark tunnels and mazelike hallways, and through open spaces riddled with ladders, ropes, and gears, all of which had their own scents, decay, sawdust, mold, and grease, though the smell of fresh paint nearly overrode the rest.

In the darkness, I tripped over a folding chair, then a card table whose leg folded under it. Dark objects hanging above us, unrecognizable in the darkness, seemed to move, which made me think of ghosts, zombies, or bats. Armies of each. When I heard a squeak, I bit my lip, so as not to scream. I'd been scaring myself.

My eyes began adjusting to the darkness as we started climbing the steps toward the dressing rooms at the half level.

We didn't dare flip on a switch, but Kyle unerringly opened the door to his mother's private dressing room. That's when Dom's perfume hit me and filled me with a grief that I feared would spill forth in sobs, but I overcame the convulsing in my throat and controlled myself for Kyle's sake.

I concentrated on my senses, the click-drip of a leaky air conditioner. Giveaway scents: old shoes, deodorant, stage makeup, and hairspray. Lots and lots of hairspray.

Once we were all in, and the door closed, Kyle flipped on the lights.

A bit blinded by them, after the darkness of the theater proper, we shaded our eyes for a minute.

Kyle leaned against the wall when the sight of the empty room finally hit him—the place where his mother *belonged*. Like, if he couldn't find her anywhere else, she would surely be here.

But she wasn't.

He massaged a brow for a minute, a man trying to get a grip on emotion. "Mom's essence still fills the place," he said, his voice soft and not quite steady.

Eve rubbed his arm.

He pulled her into a hug and buried his face in her hair.

I wanted to say, "Hello! You don't know each other." But I needed to be gentle and try to snap him out of his funk. "Eve, I hope your hair spikes don't have too much product on them. Wouldn't want Kyle to lose an eye."

Kyle raised his head with as near to a smile as I'd seen, and he hooked an arm around my neck and kissed my brow. "I'm okay. Thanks."

The first thing I saw was a shelf lined with wigs. Red wigs, from pale to bright. And what do you know, one head form was bald. One missing red wig did not mean that the strange woman in my shop had been wearing the very same.

Amazing coincidence, though.

Just looking at the rack of costumes, radiating dry-cleaning fluid and detergent, raced my heart, my fingers itching to touch, my sanity shying away from the physi-cal and mental anguish that would come with the vi-sions I expected to endure as I learned the truth about my friend's death.

I took a step away from the emotions bursting like fireworks inside me, hot pinpricks that invaded my head and solar plexus. Where was Chakra when I needed her?

But thinking about her helped. I embraced the calm and looked more closely around me.

Cheap antique white paneling made up the walls of the room.

Against the back wall stood a rose-colored Queen
Anne dressing table with Cabriole legs, three big round
lightbulbs affixed to each side of the mirror, with a
matching boudoir chair in front of it, its seat tufted in
pink fabric.

You could hardly see the top of the dressing table because of the pots and jars of perfumes, creams, powders,
oils crowded on top of it, anything and everything to
make a woman look younger and more beautiful.

Dominique had stuck a picture of Kyle in one corner
of the mirror, and stars that were her idols in others. I bit
my lip when I saw the picture of us that she'd had the
waiter take at lunch the last time we were together.

I still couldn't believe it had been the last time.

In her own whimsical way, Dom made fun of her
profession by almost crowning her mirror with a pink
boa, so it slithered along the top and hung down both
sides.

In the mirror itself: I saw the love seat reflected
against the opposite wall, upholstered in the same allover pink fabric as the chair. "It's a nice dressing room,"
I said. "They treated her like the star she was."

"Pierpont sent her flowers before every performance,"
Kyle muttered absently.

"Eve," I said, "would you take an inventory of every
item on her dressing table, no matter how small, without
touching any of it? Don't roll so much as an eyeliner."

Kyle offered us a box of rubber gloves.

"Perfect! Wow, you came prepared to snoop. Good

for you. You've got a lot more of your mother in you than I thought."

He nodded, accepting the compliment with a raised brow and a mix of pride and sadness.

"If we touch anything," I reiterated, "we do it wearing a pair of these. Devious boy." I shook my head. "Seriously, what would your mother say? You thinking like a sneak thief makes me worry about your wicked side."

With a bit of actor in him, he gave me a nefarious look. "What would you like this wicked boy to do now?"

"Oh!" Eve's eyes widened. "Ask me. Ask me."

Twelve

About half my designs are controlled fantasy, fifteen percent are total madness and the rest are bread-and-butter designs.
—MANOLO BLAHNIK

"Eve," I snapped, "keep your suggestions to yourself until the two of you are alone. Kyle, keep an ear peeled for unusual noises, so we don't get caught, and while you're doing that, check the plumbing beneath every sink. A place this old probably has brass barrel traps, perfect for holding a pill bottle of diamonds with no interruption to water flow."

Eve responded to his double take. "She lives in a very old house, and her father, the professor, believed in teaching her and her sibs, and sometimes her lucky friends—like *moi*—how to fix what needed fixing."

"I see. Well. How typically unglamorous." Kyle sighed theatrically. "I get to play plumber."

I chuckled at his ploy for sympathy, but despite that,

I couldn't take my eyes off the costumes, all on hangers, but some on racks and others on scattered wall hooks along with headdresses.

On the floor, along one wall, stood a neat row of dancing shoes, high heels, low heels, flats, boots, all in colors and fabrics to match the outfits.

Kyle watched me eye the clothes with a mix of longing and dread. "Can you read them, Aunt, I mean, Mad? Help me find out what happened to my mother?"

His words took me by surprise; Eve too, because his comment made her catch her breath.

He looked from one of us to the other. "Mad, my mother was a witch. If I can accept that, I can accept anything. I know what you told her about yourself and your gifts. Theater people are for the most part superstitious and have faith in the otherworldly. Mom was no exception, and neither am I. She, as you know, embraced the occult. So, yes, we both believe in you."

He'd spoken in the present tense, as if his mother was still here. After I got over my surprise at his faith, and his belief system, I nodded. "Eve, come try on the costumes."

Eve paled. "I hate it when you get visions."

"Do it for me?" Kyle asked.

Eve sighed. "For you, maybe, but not in front of you."

"No, of course not," I said. "We don't want to scare him."

"Gee, thanks," Eve said. "What am I, Lady MacBleh?"

"I see, you're worried about getting naked, and I'm worried he'll freak when I zone out."

"Oh, no," Kyle said. "I'll be fine. I'm used to witnessing all kinds of crazy behavior. I'm in show biz, remember? As I said, my mother told me about your gift and what you can do. I hope you don't mind. I was the only one she felt safe confiding in, and I didn't tell a soul."

"Thanks for that," I said, squeezing his arm. "Now tell me what we've got here."

"These costumes were made for *Diamond Sands*," he said. "Only Mom has worn them for the past five years, except for Ursula the few times she went on if Mom was sick, so they *might* have a story to tell."

"Who's Ursula?"

"Mom's understudy. Ursula Uxbridge."

"Of course, the understudy. She's someone who'll profit from your mother's death. Is Ursula capable of murder?"

"Capable but probably not smart enough."

"And who's capable of stealing the diamonds?" Eve asked.

"I don't give a flying firecracker about the diamonds," Kyle said. "I want to know who killed my mother, and I want them punished."

Kyle won Eve's eternal lapdog devotion for that. People had always meant more to her than money. To me, too, for that matter, but Eve took it to extremes.

"Kyle," I said, "face the wall while Eve puts on a costume."

Hands on hips, Eve tried to stare me down. "Madeira Cutler, why can't *you* wear the costumes?" She'd whined the question, a plaintive sound I'd never quite heard from her before.

This phobia of hers about my psychic ability was the first obvious fear I'd ever seen in my fearless friend.

I sighed. "I don't mean to torture you, Eve, but when I *wear* a readable outfit, I find myself in the wearer's point of view, and I can only see what the wearer saw. If I touch an outfit that someone else is wearing, I can look around the room. You know, play sleuth?"

Eve wet her lips with her tongue and raised her chin. "And you know that because?"

"I've had both experiences," I reminded her. "Remember when I tried on that cape how frustrating my limited view of the scene in that office was? But when Sherry tried on her wedding gown while I adjusted the fit, I could tell you what was hanging on the wall opposite the woman wearing the same gown a century before. That's how I know."

"When you're having a psychometric vision," Kyle asked her, "can you walk around the room and open things?"

"No, wherever the universe plants me in a vision, I seem to be stuck there. But if I'm not stuck in the outfit, I can look everywhere. If I'm in the outfit, my point of view is limited to the wearer's point of view. Simple as that."

"I do remember your experiences, dammit." Eve clenched her fists and kicked the sofa for good measure. "Mad, I am so going to get you for this. Kyle, turn around."

"Remind me not to cross you," he said, facing the mirrored wall.

"I'm not one to have a hissy, normally, but you don't know what happens when Mad gets a vision. You'll have nightmares, I tell you."

Kyle shrugged. "I'm not scared."

"You will be." Eve put her hands on her hips. "Hey, you facing the mirror is sort of defeating the purpose, isn't it?" She took Kyle by an arm and guided him farther to the right. "The *other* wall," she explained.

I shook my head, actually able to smile at their antics, despite our purpose here. "Kyle, can you tell us about *Diamond Sands*, the story line, brief synopsis?" I asked. "You know, while I help Eve change?"

"Oh sure. It's a musical about the beginnings of the Pierpont Diamond Mines, and the family, a two-hour commercial in a way, but it's a romance, too, about the current owner's Victorian great-great-grandparents, an Australian rags to riches story, which gives it an entertaining edge."

Eve fidgeted as she buttoned herself into a mostly gold camel-hair wool Victorian autumn gown with three-quarter sleeves, circa 1883. The brocade weave of peaches outlined in brown on a rust background formed the underskirt and over bodice of the dress. The plain brown wool formed the short gathered overskirt and bustle. "Great gown," I said as I stood back.

"Hot and scary," Eve said. "So, Kyle," she added, putting off the inevitable. "People pay to see this commercial?"

"They did because Dominique DeLong played the lead," he said, still staring at the dressing room door.

"Why was the show closing then?" I asked.

"Pierce Pierpont, the bastard, put a stop to advertising practically the minute his father died. I don't think Pierce was fond of my mother. I wouldn't be surprised if he intended to end her career by closing it. But hey, maybe that's me being paranoid."

"Your mother died a suspicious death," I said. "Paranoia seems reasonable considering."

"Young Pierpont does sound like a bastard," Eve agreed, her arms crossed over the gold Victorian gown, sort of daring me to come near her.

"So tell us about the show," I said, again, so Eve would relax.

"At the time it takes place, the female lead is set to take London theaters by storm. But all that ends when she's forced to accompany her husband, falsely accused of theft, to the Australian colonies. Thinking they were doomed, they served their time but ended up saving the son of the family to whom they were indentured. They were thanked with their freedom and a monetary gift to start a new life. They bought a plot of land that surprisingly yielded a mother lode of diamonds and became the richest family in Australia."

"Sounds pretty good," Eve said. "I like a happy ending."

"Victor Pierpont, Pierce's father, was a great man. I was happy for him, and I liked and respected him. His son, not so much. The musical had a lot going for it, and my mother played the rich heroine beautifully."

"Of course she did," I whispered, wishing to hell that I'd come to see her in it. That's what I get for thinking a New York show will last forever. "Now I understand why the costumes range from rags to these gorgeous Victorian gowns."

"My mother wore the gown Eve's wearing to the cast party the night before she died," Kyle said without turning.

Eve did a slow turn toward his back. "How do you know what I'm wearing, if you can't see me? You peeked!"

"Um," Kyle said, buying time. "Shiny doorknob?"

Thirteen

Costumes are the first impression that you have of the character before they open their mouth—it really does establish who they are.
—COLLEEN ATWOOD

❧

"Get your eyes off that doorknob," Eve said, "put your hand on it, instead, turn it, and go find some coveralls or jeans in one of the other dressing rooms. You can't take sink traps apart in that suit."

"Wouldn't the police have looked in the plumbing for the diamonds?" Kyle asked.

"Maybe," I said. "Maybe not."

I cocked my head to one side and pursed my lips. "Ah, how long have you two been dating?"

"Funny," Eve said. "I figure it's been about what, Kyle, an hour since we first laid eyes on each other?"

"I feel like I've known you all my life," Kyle said, "if you count the ride to the Federal building."

"Right," Eve said, "I forgot that we dropped off the arch idiot."

"Eve, stop talking about Nick that way," I said. "Honestly, you'd think you were carrying a torch for him or something. You know what they say about love and hate being two sides of the same coin."

Eve faked a dry heave. "Quick, give me a barf bag."

Kyle looked entertained, and under the circumstances, he needed that. And he needed to keep busy. "Clothes for examining the depths of sink pipe traps, Kyle," I said.

"You really think the diamonds are in the plumbing?" Eve asked when his steps faded.

"No, but they could be, and he needs to be doing something."

"Ah." Then she started fidgeting with the dress ruffles. "Are you sure you should touch this gown?" She stepped as I reached. "On second thought, don't touch."

"You know, my friend, you're going to have to get over your psychic-phobia around me. I'm not going to change."

"You already did change," she pouted. "You didn't used to read vintage clothes and scare me spitless."

"That's true. I wonder what the universe has in store for me next."

"As long as it doesn't involve me. Yikes, you put your hands in my pockets. Mad? Madeira? Where did you go? I *hate* when you pop out and forget to tell me you're leaving!"

I could hear Eve calling me but she seemed far away compared to the *Mod Squad* living room in which I found myself. Seventies striped walls in blue, lime, turquoise, and mauve, a modern half sofa with huge, almost-bouncing 3D-type polka dots and rings in nearly the same colors. Close enough in colors not to make me seasick, anyway.

The whomp-whir of a Hula-hoop snaked in and out of my peripheral vision. Had I gone back in time, or had someone failed to move with the times?

The scope of the picture didn't matter. I knew one more thing about my visions. I could look behind and around me but I couldn't see around corners. That kept me from seeing who was using the hoop. I assumed it was a teenager.

I saw Dominique's face exactly as I remembered her from our December lunch as she looked at pictures in a scrapbook, mostly of her with a handsome, mature man, arm in arm, smiling at each other and for the camera.

So this was her rather recently and not back in time. However, just to complicate matters, she was wearing the rust-and-gold brocade Victorian gown, but why she'd dress in costume, in a seventies den, during the new millennium, I couldn't imagine.

Unless the den was a set here in the theater. But the biggest oddity was the Hula-hoop. I'd heard there was a resurgence of use for exercise and physical therapy, but it didn't fit the scene, despite the fact that I stood in the midst of it.

"So why did you call me over in the middle of an obsessively unnecessary dress rehearsal?" she asked the person around the corner, the one wielding the green-striped hoop.

"Your director is a nutcase," came a strange raspy voice from the Hula-hoop corner. A voice some might consider a threat.

It reminded me of old Mrs. Thompson after her throat surgery.

"I called you because I had a brilliant idea," Deep Throat said. "I think we should steal the diamonds you wear in the play and run away together. Live life to the full, no holds barred. It's about time we came out of the closet."

Yikes, I thought. Didn't see that coming. The speaker, aka the Hula-hoop user, could have been male or female, young or old, but he/she remained around that corner and *out* of my line of vision.

Sure, I could look all around the room, even behind me, because *I* wasn't wearing the dress inciting the vision, but I still couldn't propel myself, nor the object of my vision, into my line of sight. Scrap!

"I love you, but you're nuts," Dominique told Deep Throat. Love? Really? "We'd never get away with stealing the diamonds," she declared. "And you know it."

"Sure we would. Who'd suspect us of all people?

Now that my throat cancer is gone, we could go any-where, travel the world," he/she rasped.

"Why bother stealing them?" Dom asked.

"Just for the fun of pissing off that greedy phony. He's just like his mother. We'll leave a tell-all note and leave Kyle to run the show. You did a good job with that boy, Dom. I'm proud of him."

"You should be. He's just like you."

Huh? What? They were feeding me puzzle pieces that didn't fit, or they fit a different puzzle than the one I was trying to put together.

Someone grabbed me and pushed me, face-first, against a wall. I thought tobacco voice had caught me in-vading his seventies den. I mean, Dominique would have known me, so it had to be the room's other occupant.

Then I began to focus from without, rather than from within, and the water stain in the shape of New Hamp-shire caused by the likewise-seventies air conditioner was replaced by Eve standing in front of me, shaking me until my teeth rattled.

I caught her in a bear hug. "Eve, I'm so glad it's you." Unfortunately, by hugging her, I grasped the dress again and put myself into a different vision surrounding the same dress.

I found myself backstage this time, curtain closed, lights on, and from the conversation around me, this was an after-show party, which is why the cast was still in costume.

The actor dressed like a traveling preacher hit a gong

and waited for silence to speak. "Pierpont the younger has something to say," the actor announced, and a handsome man dressed in an uber-expensive suit climbed a set of five stairs to tower over us and rock on his heels, hands behind his back. Wielding power and reveling in it.

Even though the news must be bad, he rode the rising wave until his toadies stirred and shifted, out of patience.

"I'll get right to it," he said. *Too late.* "You're good at what you do. Talented. You put on a hell of a show, but we're not making a profit, and let's face it, we're not in the business to lose money."

The cast groaned. Their expressions of horror told the story. They knew what was coming.

"Tomorrow night will be our last performance," Pierpont the younger said. "We're closing the show."

I guessed that this was a pre-cancel-the-show party.

The company broke up while the grumbling in general continued. Pierpont descended the steps, head higher, if that were possible, and disappeared into a dark hall.

Dom—or, I, in Dom's body—headed for her dressing room, but she stopped when she saw her ex-husband close himself in her leading man's dressing room.

"Ma-dei-ra!" She shook me and I went limp, my focus returning to the present.

"Eve! You hit me."

"You wigged out again, and we're no longer alone in the theater. Get me out of this thing. It's like the dress that ate Chicago. No, I'm a nutcase, you'll sail off to la-la land if you do. Don't touch it. I'll get out of it on my own. If you leave me, again, I might have to beat you."

"Good start," I said, rubbing my cheek. Then I heard footsteps and voices. "I wonder what happened to Kyle."

"Damn, there's no time to find out or change. Let's just get the hell out of Oz." Still wearing the dress, Eve pried open the door and peeked out while panic shivered through me and I grabbed a black trench coat off a door hook to conceal my red suit and make myself less conspicuous.

I barely took a step before I knew that I should never act in panic, especially when it came to donning a piece of unknown clothing. Dumb, dumb, dumb. My head ached like a shimmer of rising desert heat, and I no longer stood in Dom's dressing room. Instead, I stood just outside said room, carefully opening the door a silent crack.

Dom paced while the unaddressed box that came to me carrying the seafoam gown sat on the floor beside her purse. She glanced at the door, and I leaned back, so not even my shadow could cross her threshold. Then she looked furtively around her dressing room before she glanced back at the door. The theater seemed as dark and deserted on that occasion as it had upon our arrival.

After seeming certain she was alone, she took a small

glass jar of clear gel-type liquid from her purse and switched it with the one already on her dressing table.

Satisfied that I'd witnessed the switch, though not sure why, I shut Dom's dressing room door as silently and successfully as I'd opened it, and I came back to myself. It happened so fast, I felt like the door changed places with me.

"Mad!" Eve pulled on my arm. "Are you coming? The voices are getting closer."

I shed the trench coat like it was made of spiders.

Succumbing to desperate times, I grabbed a black opera cloak from the costume rack, long enough to hide my red shoes, aware this time that it might be a vision maker.

I raised the hood to hide the cinnamon highlights in my hair and found myself wishing for a certain wizard's invisibility cloak. Fiction aside, this was as close as I could get to blending with the unlit theater.

God forbid the cloak had something to say; it should speak fast, because our time alone was coming to an end.

I turned off the light, pushed Eve from the dressing room, and urged her away from the approaching footsteps. Problem: We didn't know where the hell we were going, and not so much as a glimmer lit the end of this tunnel.

We did, however, find a ladder. "Climb," I said.

Eve whimpered.

We ended up crawling along a wide paint-stained

plank walkway above a bottomless black well that might be a stage or a crocodile pit. Note to me: cloaks, not made for crawling; cloaks made for idiots. After catching myself up short with it, I grabbed the two bottom corners, one in each fist, and continued across the plank.

"Madeira Cutler," Eve whispered right behind me, her whisper shaky though she meant to be strong. "You get me into the stupidest trouble."

I turned to her. "Really? Like crawling the peak of your father's garage at age seven to catch a baby squirrel?"

"Shut up!"

"I love you, too. Now shush."

Sometime later, I was going down a safer ladder than I had climbed at the beginning of this crazy trek. I found myself behind a curtain, Eve no longer behind me. Had she not followed me down?

When had we parted ways?

I squeaked when a man in a clean but tattered Victorian suit took my arm and led me to the center of a seemingly empty room, shadows dancing, light to dark and back, again, as my eyes adjusted to the darkness. "Who are you?" I asked. *A dead actor was my guess.*

"Your husband, of course."

So . . . my leading man, perhaps, once upon a time?

"There," he said, pointing to the outline of a body on the floor. "That's where you lost your beauty and died." He gave me a double take. "But you have your beauty back."

Ah, Dom would like that, keeping her beauty for eternity and not having to age in the public eye. But I was losing track of my purpose. I'd never conversed with a vision before, so I should make the best of it.

"I might still have my beauty," I told this phantom husband of mine, "but I lost the diamonds." *Yes, I was baiting him, trying to draw him out.*

"So everyone thinks," said he, "but you still have them, don't you?"

"Do I?" In my experience with Dante, I had concluded that ghosts had no reason to lie. But maybe this specter was delusional.

I realized that Dominique had died in this very spot, and I got dizzy again, my world seeming to tilt and flip entirely, my viewpoint coming from somewhere near the ceiling, the stage below me.

I tried not to look but, despite myself, I stared down at the outline of Dominique's body in the center of the stage floor.

Grief overwhelmed me.

Someone held me while I cried and stood me upright again. Above me, the ceiling. Below me, that terrible stage floor with the chalk outline of Dom's body.

"Nick!" I said when I realized those were his arms around me, him consoling me, or maybe I knew all along.

As we stood there, he grabbed a cord with a switch at the end, and the curtains parted with a "whoosh" of sweeping purple velvet, thick silk red and gold tassels bobbing with the movement.

Eve stood on the audience side of the open curtain still wearing the gold Victorian gown. Beside her, Kyle looked dapper in torn jeans and a black V-neck T-shirt, the two of them handcuffed together.

Fourteen

He who would travel happily must travel light.
—ANTOINE DE SAINT-EXUPÉRY

"Are you all right?" Nick asked looking me over like I was a prized porcelain figurine.

I pushed back the cloak's hood to reveal my face and hair. "I'm fine."

"Good," Nick said. "Now I can beat you."

I shook out my hair. "How did you find us?"

"I called Higgins to pick me up, and he told me where he was waiting for three idiots—my words, not his. I had one of the guys from the New York office drop me in front of the theater, and after he left, I came after you by myself."

"Thank God."

"No, thank Nick," Nick said. "Come here, you two putzes," he told Eve and Kyle. "Do you know how much trouble Mad can get you into?"

"Hey?"

Eve opened her mouth and Nick gave her a warning look.

"Let me rephrase that," Nick said. "Kyle, do you know how much trouble Eve and Mad can get you into?"

Kyle winked at Eve, but he was wise enough not to tick off Nick, as he, our so-called rescuer, unlocked the cuffs.

When Kyle and Eve were free, Nick rubbed his nose, his eyes bright with amusement. "Go find your own clothes and leave the stolen costumes where they were. No more nosing around on your own." He narrowed his eyes my way. "This is a murder investigation."

Eve and Kyle left, but Nick didn't let me go. As a matter of fact, he held on tighter, making me feel cherished, important. We rarely did that in this relationship, held tight. Too dangerous, clinging.

"You've been trying to read vintage clothes again," he said.

"I think I've been hallucinating, instead. Not much I saw made sense. And I've never had a historical character, or a ghost, in a vision, converse with me. It was like Hogwarts set in Oz narrated by Doctor Who."

"Serves you right. Go put that cloak away and let's get you out of here. Kyle has a schedule to keep, even if *he's* too polite to say so."

We were a quiet group getting back into the limo, but I managed to smuggle a black trench coat with a nefarious past in one of Dom's big old Marc Jacobs purses, my own purse also stuffed inside, and pass it off as mine. The coat had been worn by someone spying on Dominique, and I needed to find out what else it could tell me.

Nick didn't even notice.

To my surprise, Higgins took us to a forensics morgue. "I thought we were supposed to go straight to Dominique's," I said.

"I'm sorry, Mad," Kyle said, guilt skewing his "I'm okay" expression. "I couldn't do this alone," he admitted.

"Do what alone?" I asked, dreading the answer.

"Identify Mom's body."

Higgins turned in his seat, his face a mask of concern. "Young Mr. DeLong needs a friend. Everybody else in his life right now wants something. He needs someone willing to give rather than take."

"I'm here for you, Kyle," I said, squeezing his arm.

"Let's go inside," Nick said. "Higgins, thanks for putting Kyle's situation into perspective for us."

"Thank you," Kyle said, speaking to everyone but no one.

One by one, we were given IDs in a sterile, nondescript lobby, and when the elevator doors closed us in, Nick took me in his arms. "Prepare yourself, ladybug. You, too, Kyle."

"What's a forensics morgue?" I asked, never having heard the distinction.

Nick examined the toes of his dress shoes and slipped

a hand in one pocket. "Let's just say that Dominique would be in a regular morgue, if the law didn't think she died under mysterious circumstances."

I nodded, my throat too tight to speak.

With every floor the elevator climbed came a stronger smell of disinfectant.

We got out on the sixth floor where no amount of the stuff would be able to cover the smell of death.

Kyle began to pace the length of the mahogany-trim waiting room, circa 1930. Hands behind his back, he was so focused on the black-and-white floor tiles, he seemed to forget our existence.

"Kyle," I said. "Why didn't you identify your mom last night?"

He closed the space between us and wrapped his arms around me, his body wracked with one tightly wound shiver. "That would have made it real."

I had no control over the sob that rose in me.

Maybe I *was* older than him, after all. On the other hand, maybe when we lose our mother, we're all ten years old inside.

"Jaconetti?" a suit across the room called. "Is that you? I heard you were in town today."

A couple of men in FBI-type suits came to shake Nick's hand. "Did the Bureau send you?" a fed with a buzz cut asked.

Nick performed the introductions, but I was so freaked at being in a forensics morgue, Dom's body stiff and cold nearby, I keyed into Kyle's fear of making it real.

Foul play had contributed to Dominique's death, I thought, absorbing the info, maybe for the first time, and as I did, I saw her switching those jars. Why?

Then I realized the intros were over and I had no names to put with faces. So I examined Nick's cronies, specifically their hair, or their lack thereof, and dubbed them Buzz and Shinola.

"DeLong," Buzz said to Kyle. "So you're family? My condolences. We're looking into the lost diamonds. The boys in blue over there are investigating cause of death. Don't worry. We'll compare notes."

Hah. I knew from Nick and Werner that these two diverse arms of the law both wanted to come out on top. Both wanted to be the ones who solved the case. In other words, they wouldn't like sharing info, and there would be no fraternizing without persuasion.

Nick gave me a reassuring look. I gave him a trusting nod.

A woman in medical whites came out and motioned Kyle forward. He hesitated, looked back at me, and I took his arm to accompany him into a smaller office.

When we got there, Nick came up beside us.

Eve waved through the glass from beside the elevator. I didn't blame her for standing as far back as she could.

The assistant medical examiner, according to her badge, showed us a photograph that I didn't at first recognize.

When I did, I found myself floaty and leaning hard into Nick at my back, his hands tight on my arms. He squeezed them harder and harder. The uncomfortable constriction was the only thing that kept me from passing out. Smart fed.

"Can we have a glass of water over here?" he asked.

Man, he knew me well.

Even as I sipped the water, I tried to talk myself out of floating to the floor in blessed oblivion. This is not about you, Cutler, I told myself. Get a grip.

In the photograph, the blotches on Dominique's face ranged from burgundy to purple, the skin around her eyes the worse, her nose, cheeks, and lips triple their normal size.

That ghost hadn't been kidding. She had lost her earthly beauty in a very big way. Sadness took over my weakness and the sight of her made me mad. I was gonna find the sonofabitch who did this to my friend.

Kyle cleared his throat more than once and swallowed hard before he could get his jaw to work. "She looks like she was stung by bees."

"Can you give me a positive ID?" the woman asked. "Is this Dominique DeLong?"

"Yes," Kyle said with a catch in his voice. "That's her."

"And you are?" the examiner queried, as she filled out a form.

"Kyle DeLong, her son. May I ask what killed her?"

"I'm sorry. It's not up to me to say. I do the preliminary lab report. My boss does the official medical examiner's report. The FBI and the police put that together with officers' and detectives' reports, witness statements, and evidence, and then *maybe* they tell you what happened."

I tore my gaze from my poor beautiful friend's marred face. "But you do think it was murder?"

"It doesn't matter what I think, Ms. DeLong."

I didn't correct her assumption that I was family. What did it matter?

She turned to Kyle. "I can tell you that with your ID of the deceased, we've finished and we'll be releasing Ms. DeLong to the funeral home within the hour."

"Good," Kyle said. "I made arrangements this morning." He took out his cell phone and called the funeral parlor. Closing it, he said, "The wake and interment service are tomorrow."

"Why so soon?" I asked.

"I want it dignified. It'll be more respectful and less like a circus, if we keep the spectators down to a minimum. The longer we take, the more fans show up."

"Right. Of course."

Nick continued to hold me as we went to meet Eve in the waiting room. "Who would want to harm Dominique?" I asked.

Kyle made a mocking sound. "I'm afraid the list is as long as my arm." Then he opened that arm, and Eve walked into it.

Fifteen

They came as if there might never be anything like it again:
They were in mod clothes, Victorian suits, and granny gowns,
old west outfits, pirate costumes . . .   —CHARLES PERRY

❧

The doorbell to Dom's Fifth Avenue mansion overlooking Central Park began to ring at seven, and frankly I feared that it would never stop.

The characters who came to offer Kyle their condolences outlandishly attempted to outdress each other, and would once have been called the "radical chic."

At another time in fashion history, the faux-grieving rubberneckers vying for a glimpse at the twisted steel of Dom's metaphorical but deadly "car accident" were known as Bohemians.

As far as I was concerned, they were slimy, scaled predators leapfrogging each other to reach the lower rungs of the ladder to success.

However typed, there were some legitimate artists

and designers, interspersed with leeches and, for the most part, no-talent hangers-on. Some had genius, some had style, but most had their claws bared in one form or another in an industry that chewed up wannabes and spit them on dirty sidewalks to be tread upon by the uncaring hordes.

Speaking of which, I'd managed to secure my brother-in-law's family home, Cortland House in Mystick Falls as the venue for the Dominique DeLong Memorial Vintage Fashion Show for charity. Hordes would attend that, too, just to get a look at Dominique's things, not to mention getting inside the gaudy Vancortland palace, which, to be fair, my sister's husband hated, though that's where he was brought up.

Kyle pulled all the right strings so that Dom's vintage collection fashion show would be advertised in the news tomorrow, along with all the gory details of her death.

It seemed irreverent, but Dom herself had said she wanted it done while she was still news. So I went ahead and set it up.

I sighed and looked around, feeling like I'd become one of them.

To think that someone in this room might have killed Dom for money, or sport, or for a step up that infamous ladder with the razor sharp rungs.

I saw very few signs of sincere grief, except in one poor soul weeping in the guest bath off the foyer. "Can I get you a glass of water or something stronger?" I asked.

"Oh!" She wiped her eyes with a tissue as if she shouldn't have been caught there. "No, thank you. I just . . . miss her. We talked, her and I, about everything."

"I'm sorry," I said, extending my hand. "I should introduce myself. Maddie Cutler. I'm a friend of Dom's."

The grief-stricken woman's eyes widened and she curtseyed. "Ms. Cutler, I'm Ms. DeLong's personal maid, Kerri O'Day, and I'll be at your service while you're here. They've given you her room, you see. It's not my place to grieve openly so I apologize."

"Well, Kerri, I find it refreshing to see someone other than her son and I grieving. Feel free to let your feelings show. I respect you for them. Do you think that you might be up to answering some questions about Ms. DeLong later?"

The freckle-faced girl curtseyed again. "Thank you, Ms. Cutler. Of course."

I hooked my arm through hers. "Don't ruin your knees on my account with curtseys. I've never had a maid in my life. No need to wait on me. Think of me as a friend. We have something in common, our friendship with Dom."

Kerri looked around as if someone might have heard, and when no one pounced, she nodded.

"Are there any other friends of Dominique's here?"

Kerri leaned close. "In name or in truth?"

"People who *really* cared about her."

"Phoebe and Mr. Kyle care, as you said. Higgins, in his own way. Not many, miss."

"Mad. Call me Mad or Maddie."

"You shouldn't be seen with me, miss," she whispered.

I watched her open a door that I presumed led to the service stairs.

Kerri had confirmed my suspicions. People were here to gossip or rub elbows with the stars and probably for food and champagne. Indeed, some acted like this was a celebration, instead of a time when condolences and consolation were called for.

The person or persons, however, who most interested me, were the one or two who might be here to make sure that Dominique DeLong was really dead.

First in line in the making-sure department, Ursula Uxbridge, Dominique's understudy, held court dressed to be seen in a frothy black Oscar de la Renta paired with shiny red Casadei heels. Overdress too much?

I had managed to change in the downstairs powder room from the red suit into a little black dress a la *Sabrina* by Givenchy with racy David Evans platform slingbacks. I managed to grab a chatelaine finger purse with a lipstick in it before Higgins took our bags upstairs.

I caught Ursula alone and spoke to her before introducing myself. "Do you think that Dominique will actually be missed?" I asked.

A sly one, Ursula hesitated long enough to mentally calculate her answer while she assessed whether I could move her career forward or not. If she decided not, her answer wouldn't matter at all, and we both knew it.

"Dominique will be a hard act to follow," Ursula said

diplomatically. "But I'll do my best to live up to her talent and make her proud."

It was all I could do not to applaud. As for grief, that never entered her shrewd expression. "Well played," I said, clinking champagne glasses with her, and I walked away.

I worked the room while some of the men and women in blue stood on the sidelines with full plates, adding suspects to their lists. Others openly questioned the guests.

Nick ignored his FBI buds for the wannabe models, or actresses, or both, all of them drooling over him. I figured it happened all the time when he was on assignment, him charming a bevy of babes so they'd spill national secrets, or so I'd always imagined.

Didn't mean I had to like it. I shouldn't be jealous, though. He was simply grilling them in his own hunkalicious way.

We were free agents after all, on or off. Didn't mean he had to flaunt it.

Afraid I'd go for some cat's throat, I went to sit beside Kyle on the sofa.

Considering the size of the crowd who were supposed to be offering their sympathies, him sitting alone with Eve was nothing short of narcissism on the part of his visitors.

Eve leaned intimately over Kyle toward me, so he had a good view of her cleavage. "Hey, Mad," she asked, "want me to handle Nick? You know, break it up?"

"Break what up?" I asked, as if I hadn't noticed.

"Boy toy's harem, of course. You're green and you know it. Let me take care of it, please? It'll be fun."

I gave her a half nod, so I'd only feel half guilty.

She winked. "Don't worry, it won't hurt a bit."

Sixteen

Beauty is in the eye of the beholder and it may be necessary
from time to time to give a stupid or misinformed beholder a
black eye.
           —MISS PIGGY

"Poor Nick," Kyle said. "What do you think she'll do
to him?"

"God only knows, but she can't stand him, so if she
cozies up to him, don't think anything of it."

She got in Nick's face. "You bastard," she hissed.
"Playing the field, again, in front of everyone, flaunting
your infidelity."

What an actress.

"Eve," Nick said, rolling his eyes.

Eve made a motion like she was going to knee him,
just to scare him, but the heel snapped on her vintage
lace-up boots, and she started to fall.

Failing to regain her balance, her other leg went up as
she went down, and she kicked Nick in the crotch.

Ack! I clapped a hand over my mouth.

I didn't know what was worse. Nick getting kicked in the nads or Eve ending up on her assets.

Nick firmed his spine, but I could see his lips turn white as he scowled.

Kyle swallowed. "I didn't think she'd do that."

I shook my head, because neither had I, and I couldn't seem to find my voice.

Eve stood up, clumsy as a drunk skank. "Testosterone spill, aisle five!" she said as she limped quickly and ungracefully out the door.

Nick turned, slowly and carefully, and followed her, with pretty much the same staggering gait.

"Oh God," I said. "He's gonna kill her!"

Kyle rose as if to the rescue. "Then I hope she starts running when she hits the foyer."

Together we followed them from the living room.

The occupants of the room burst into chatter as we left.

The foyer stood empty, the front door open. We could hear Eve's screams getting farther away.

We found Nick on the precious but rare strip of grass at the side of the house, toward the back, bent over double, his hands on his knees, sweat on his brow and upper lip.

"I found Nick," I called to Kyle. "If you can catch Eve, tell her she can stop running now."

I bent down so my face was near Nick's. "Are you all right?"

"As soon as I wring her neck, I'm sure I'll feel better."

"She didn't mean to hurt you. Surely you know that."

"What did she mean?"

"She saw you flirting and said she'd take care of it."

He gave me a "this is your fault" look.

"Hey, I didn't know what she intended, believe me," I said. "I had plans for tonight."

"Cancel 'em."

"Damn."

He straightened, pain still etching his features. "Let's talk about something else?" He tried to straighten as he looked around. "Hey, look at the ancient ivy climbing the corner of the mansion here? Some of the thicker vines are scraped, like somebody's tried to climb them, and their foot slipped a few times. Did Kyle say the place had been broken into?"

"It hasn't," Kyle said, appproaching, Eve using him as both a crutch and a human shield.

"Meyers," Nick said.

"My heel broke. Mad, I should get a refund. I got these boots at your shop this morning."

I shook my head sadly. "Your first spiked-heel boots and they turned on you."

"I have those Fendi boots, remember? The heels weren't as sharp, but they were friendly."

"Unless you count the man you knocked unconscious with them?"

"You make a habit of this, Eve?" Nick asked.

"No," I said. "She was saving my life that time. Eve, I do owe you a refund. It was my fault, Nick, for not catching the flaw in the boots when I put them out in the shop."

Nick cringed. "For her overacting, at the least, Eve owes me two good—"

Eve stamped her single well-shod foot. "I didn't mean to kick you. Really I didn't." She giggled and Nick reached for her.

"I didn't," she said letting Kyle pull her away, "but it's kinda funny that it happened by accident when I've wanted to do it for years."

"You'll get yours when you least expect it," Nick promised. "Meanwhile, Kyle, come closer and take a look at these vines. I think you should step up your nighttime surveillance."

"Nick," Kyle said. "Is this a ploy?"

"No, seriously. Your house is in danger of being burglarized or worse. Eve, I can pay back anytime. Face it; you can't protect her in Connecticut."

"Thanks for the warning." Kyle put an arm around Eve's shoulders and held her against his side opposite Nick as we went back inside.

I did the same with Nick, also to protect Eve. "Do you need an ice pack, Jaconetti?"

Seventeen

Fashion is born by small facts, trends, or even politics, never by trying to make little pleats and furbelows, by trinkets, by clothes easy to copy, or by the shortening or lengthening of a skirt.
— ELSA SCHIAPARELLI

Nick took a right turn into the powder room off the foyer and I practically went for Eve's throat. "Why would you do that?"

"The heel broke and I slipped. I *intended* to scare him but I unfortunately scared him by losing my balance, which made him buck dangerously forward. Honestly, I only meant to taunt him."

"You're never gonna live it down."

"He'll be out for blood, won't he?"

"I would be," Kyle said. "You don't do that often, do you?"

"Never again in my life," Eve said, her hand raised. "As Bill Gates is my witness, never again."

"Says the computer genius." I shook my head. "Let's

go back inside so Nick won't be so embarrassed when he comes out of the powder room."

Eve giggled.

"Steampunk brat, you gotta stop that."

"I know," she said trying to look contrite. "It was an accident, but like a dream come true, you know?"

"I know *you*, all too well, unfortunately."

We stopped as we reached the parlor.

As if Ursula owned the place, or soon would, she was playing hostess in Dom's house, working the bright cabbage-rose room of Victorian antiques, as she crossed a red oriental carpet outlined in roses.

I leaned into Kyle. "Is Ursula one of the Parasites?"

He tilted his head. "She might not head the noxious cyborgs, but she's certainly the most enthusiastic," he whispered. "She's starring in *Diamond Sands'* late show tonight."

"What?" Eve asked from Kyle's other side. "Your mother's show? Ursula's going to play Dominique's role the night after she died?"

"She *is* Dom's understudy," I said, "but Pierpont should be closing the theater for a couple of days out of respect for Dom's memory."

Kyle shrugged. "They closed it for the early show today, which I guess is something, but in a few hours, it'll be business as usual. Not Pierpont's fault really. The public stormed the ticket office this morning, and instead of giving refunds, they ended up selling tickets. Tonight they'll have the biggest audience since

Diamond Sands opened, and Ursula will be its new star."

"Or its newest flop," Eve said. "I vote for her to flop."

"It probably won't flop now," I said. "That will always be the play in which the leading lady actually did die in the last act. Ursula won't even have to be good. The show will go on." I sighed. "I think the world will always want to see a car wreck or the aftermath."

"Gruesome as it sounds, they will," Eve said, accepting a champagne flute. "Like right now, I'm watching for Nick."

"You," I said. "You step in where Satan fears to tread."

"Like us in the theater, today?" Kyle asked.

"That was different," I explained. "We were looking for clues to your mother's death, not gossip, but a trail of blood, or—" I gave Eve a pointed look. "Signs of suffering."

Eve sipped her drink. "At least the people who go to the theater tonight won't be breaking in the way we did."

"Chill, Meyers," I said. "If you were a cat, you wouldn't have a whole life left. And you'd best keep my secrets, because I know yours."

She leaned into Kyle. "I know her secrets, too."

Kyle pointed at me with his chin. "But I'm thinking Mad has more lives left than you do." He caught us in a playful headlock, one on each side of him, and pulled us close. "Thanks for making me smile," he said, his voice raw and raspy as he let us go.

"You mean I entertained you when I assaulted Nick?"

"Hell no. *That* will give me nightmares."

I had to stifle a giggle. Sure, Kyle was younger than us, but Dominique had done a great job raising him. Good company, and honest about his feelings, he was easy to stand beside in a crisis. I felt for him. Hell, *I* could barely stop thinking about never seeing Dominique again. How must he feel about never seeing his mother again?

Well, baste it; I knew the answer to that. The sad fact was that he'd never get over losing his mother.

Eve gave Kyle a sip of her champagne, and I wondered if their attraction would outlast our visit.

"Is Pierpont providing fresh diamonds for tonight's show?" I asked.

Kyle nodded. "Ursula said they are. Can't blame the company for trying. A new and successful run for the show could be their shot at recouping months' worth of lost profits. As for the diamonds, whether they're found or not, there'll be no loss there, thanks to the magic of insurance."

Kyle shrugged. "I heard there'd be extra men guarding the diamonds tonight."

"Not the actress," I muttered. "Just the diamonds."

Eighteen

In an epoch as somber as ours, one must fight for luxury inch
by inch.
                                                    —CHRISTIAN DIOR

A woman, unknown to me, made a grand entrance into
Dom's living room, and she really caught my attention.
"Who's the brunette with the flowing mermaid hair?"

"You mean the mermaid my ex-father is following
with his eyes while hitting on someone else?"

"Ian DeLong is your *ex*-father?"

"Yeah, when he left Mom for another woman, I said
if he was her ex, he was mine, too. Mom and I called
him my ex-dad from that day on."

I chuckled. "I do believe he's hit on every female
without an oxygen tank, except for me and Eve."

"Only because you're with me," Kyle said. "Otherwise, you'd both have your chance. Good old dad. His
current target used to be Mom's catty "best friend.""

Kyle made quotes in the air when he said best friend. "Her name is Quinny Veneble. She's got money but not enough to hold Ian DeLong's attention."

"Quinny?" I chuckled.

"Silly name but it fits," Kyle said.

"And the brassy blonde Ian's watching?" I asked.

"That's Phoebe Muir, Quinny's daughter. I like Phoebe. She was my mother's secretary, assistant, confidant, an all-around girl Friday, on and offstage, twenty-four-seven."

"That arrangement smacks of nepotism." I didn't mean to be rude. The observation just slipped out.

"Depends on your point of view. Quinny wasn't happy when Mom hired Phoebe. She wanted her daughter to marry rich and become a society queen, not work for her mother's richer, more popular, and more famous 'best friend.'"

Phoebe's flawless complexion caught my imagination, like I'd seen it someplace before. I wondered what it would look like with bright red curls falling to her shoulders rather than that mermaid hair falling down her back. Tonight she wore an emerald green Carolina Herrera gown, but I could easily imagine her in a red Versace cape.

"Didn't anybody get the memo that this isn't the Oscars?" I asked Kyle.

"In this circle, any chance to show off is Oscar night."

"You know what," I said. "I haven't met your mother's leading man, yet."

"Lance Taggart. I haven't seen him, tonight, either."

"Your mother must pay Phoebe well if she can afford designer clothes."

"No, Phoebe's mother Quinny pays her well, *in* clothes," Kyle said. "But Phoebe would rather live with us. She has an apartment upstairs in the servant's attic quarters."

"Any of the other parasites live here?"

"Sure. Mom's chef, Zander Pollock. He wanted Mom to set him up in business and get him his own TV cooking show."

I sat straighter. "Was he angry at your mother when she didn't do what he wanted?"

"Mighty angry. I heard them arguing."

Feeling like Werner, I made a note of that. "Did he threaten her?"

"No, only her food."

"That's significant. Any other suspects in residence?"

"Mom's makeup artist and hairdresser, Rainbow Joy. Daughter of a flower child. Not fond of what she calls the upper classes. Rainbow Joy likes to read self-help books and dole out the advice, her earth-child version of it, that is, whether you want to hear it or not."

"Any of the leeches in residence strike you as suspects?"

"All of them, including my ex-father, though he doesn't live here. But don't limit your expectations. You haven't met all the Parasites, yet.

"Like who?" I asked.

"Like . . . Galina Lockhart," Kyle said watching Ursula Uxbridge. "Galina was Mom's biggest rival. She wanted Mom's part in *Diamond Sands*, and never forgave Mom for getting it. Hell, Galina's always wanted anything Mom had."

"Sounds like a sweetie."

"I'll point her out when I see her. She doesn't seem to be here tonight, but watch the way she and my ex-dad look at each other. There's chemistry; I just don't know if they ever made a toxic mix of it. Just watch the people who actually "pose" beside the casket tomorrow. You'll find Galina, eventually."

My eyes filled despite myself. Dominique DeLong in a casket.

I thought the guests would never leave, especially Ian, who acted as if he owned the Gothic white-granite showplace and that everyone was there to see him instead of Kyle. Fact was, Dominique got the Fifth Avenue mansion in the divorce settlement.

One thing I already knew about Ian is that he never went anywhere without a glass of Scotch in his hand. And when he held a glass, the very crooked baby finger on his right hand became more noticeable. The pinky curved right then back toward the left and pointed to the rest of his hand.

Kyle's little finger did not resemble his ex-father's, but one of the Parasites had a little finger that did.

Nineteen

Eventually everything connects—people, ideas, objects. The quality of the connections is the key . . .—CHARLES EAMES

❧

The genetic crooked baby-finger thing didn't prove that Kyle wasn't Ian DeLong's. But it sure made me question the paternity of another member of the Parasites.

So . . . had Ian fathered another child? If so, did that speak to motive? Possibly, so I guessed it was worth questioning all three: potential mother, father, and child. Meanwhile, useless speculation had no bearing on the immediate facts surrounding Dom's death.

I'd save my curiosity for opportunities to speak to each of them separately, and by separate, I meant alone and one-on-one, without the others in the vicinity.

Still, the coincidence bugged me, and I turned to Kyle. "Who exactly did your dad leave your mother for?"

Kyle shrugged. "You know, we never found out. He's

such a player, it could have been a number of women, and he never married after the divorce."

Note to me. Find out who Ian DeLong fooled around with. Oh, yeah, I already knew: anyone who wore a skirt.

I needed to mingle, but I was too tired for intelligent speech. I longed to discuss my ideas about Dominique's death with someone, preferably Nick. My head was spinning and I knew talking would help me clarify my thoughts. Nick had texted me that he'd returned to FBI headquarters after the "kneeing" incident, and he still hadn't returned by the time the household retired.

That's when I learned that they put Nick and me in separate bedrooms on different floors. Great. I wanted to talk to him and to make sure he wasn't permanently disabled.

Kyle had given me Dom's room, so I could look around, and frankly, I avoided the closet. That's how tired I was. I was avoiding clothes altogether.

Making myself at home in Dominique's bedroom made me miss her something fierce. I curled up in her boudoir chair, the stuffed bunny from her bed in my arms, and I had a good cry.

When Nick slipped into my room around midnight I was surprised my inelegant sobs didn't scare him away. His expression turned to concern when he saw me, then he was there, picking me up and carrying me to the bed.

He kicked off his shoes, loosened his tie, and we sat against the headboard while he held me and let me cry and talk about Dom and my impressions of the Parasites.

"Feel better?" he asked when I went silent.

"I do. Thank you. How about you?"

"Embarrassed as hell. Where's Eve?" Nick asked. "I was hoping you'd be bunking together so I could beat her."

"Her room's on the same floor as Kyle's, big surprise, but yours is two floors up."

"Eve's influence, no doubt. Never mind, I'll find my room first thing in the morning when I need a change of clothes."

I wiped my tears, loving the feel of being in Nick's arms after so long, my big, sturdy fed with the colorful silk boxers hidden beneath the deceptive dignity of his black suit, though that dignity had been impugned tonight, and I should remember to treat him gently and not expect much.

"I know that you've talked to the police and the FBI, Nick. What did Dominique die of?"

Nick kissed my brow. "There's no official medical examiner's report, yet."

"Nick," I begged.

"The forensics investigation being over doesn't mean the crime's been solved, ladybug."

"How did she die, dammit?"

"The police and the Feds combed the dressing rooms and stage last night, checking under every splinter for the diamonds or some kind of murder weapon."

"Whatever that might be," I said. "Stop stalling."

Nick hesitated as if trying to choose his words while he swirled my hair around his finger. "It appears she died of anaphylactic shock. She had a fatal allergic reaction to something."

"Peanuts?"

"Yes! They found traces in her bloodstream. I take it that was an issue?"

"God yes. But that's impossible. Dominique would never go near a peanut. She was so allergic that you couldn't touch a peanut, then touch her because the imprint of your finger would welt up on her skin."

"That's insane."

"Some people are that allergic. I know because she told me that Kyle did that to her once when he was a kid. He'd had a peanut butter sandwich at nursery school. After he touched her cheek, not only did she welt up, her throat closed and she was rushed to the hospital."

"So that's why she had her own cook," Nick speculated.

It still didn't make sense. "That doesn't explain what happened to her face."

He stood and unbuttoned his shirt. "There were traces of peanut oil in the welts on her face, Mad, hence the swelling. So that's how the poison entered, through her facial pores."

"What? She got splashed with peanut soup?"

"I didn't say it made sense, which is why the case

hasn't been solved. I'm just telling you what the cops got from the preliminary forensics report."

"And what about the diamonds? Was she killed for them? Are they connected?"

"Nobody's sure, but we're keeping a watchful eye on her lover, from a distance for the moment."

Twenty

There is only one gift you should accept on your first date—
diamonds.   —MISS PIGGY

❧

"Dominique had a lover?"

"A young lover."

I sat forward. "In other words, she paraded him around?"

"Yes, but they kept it cozy and private, and she had nothing to say about him to the press. No one can even find a picture of him facing the camera."

I chuckled. "He wasn't her lover. She hired him to bolster her image. Sexy actress flaunts boy toy. It's called publicity, Jaconetti."

"Well, her toy's a suspicious character, who we're watching. Gregor Zukovski, from a small Slavic country. He's *known* to the Bureau and every other intelligence agency. We suspect he might have taken the diamonds for terrorist purposes."

"Oh, I hope I'm wrong about her hiring him, then. Would he have poisoned Dom to get them?"

"Yes, but one wonders why he would murder her in public."

"So he was nowhere near her when it happened," I said, "which pretty much makes the Parasites, and anybody who worked at the theater, suspect."

"Right. Problem with Zukovski is that he knows every government employee in the tri-state area. So, if he gets on a plane, the Bureau has asked me to get on it with him."

"That's dangerous."

"Nothing new, and you know it. That's my job, ladybug."

"I didn't need it confirmed, thanks, today of all days."

"If I can find the diamonds while we're still in United States airspace, I can take them and Zukovski back with me."

Damn. Seducing Nick to keep him safe wouldn't work. He'd recently had a run-in with a live nutcracker. "I might need you here," I whispered. "This is difficult for me."

"Yes, you've lost your friend, but you're the most independent and least needy person I know. Don't try to give me the guilts. It won't work. Besides, I'm here now." Nick's eyes smoldered and he leaned my way.

"Don't let those bedroom eyes of yours make any promises the big boy can't keep," I whispered against his lips.

He frowned and his cell phone rang before his lips met mine.

"Tucking A!" I snapped, as he sat up to answer it.

"I'm on my way," he said a minute later. "Airport, ladybug." He slipped on his shoes. "Gregor Zukovski's on the run. Looks like he's taking the next plane to Slovenia."

"And that's where?"

"In a galaxy far away."

"You're going after the man who might have killed Dom, alone? You're chasing a possible diamond thief on his own turf?"

"I won't be alone. Your brother's waiting for me at the airport." He kissed her nose. "You didn't hear that from me, and you're not to tell a soul."

"I know the drill, you rat. You knew this was going down, or Alex wouldn't already be here."

Nick sighed, leaned over the bed, and consoled me with a practiced kiss filled with yearning. He pulled away but came back for more. "I'd hoped it wouldn't happen for at least an hour."

"Fat lot of good that would have done us." I walked him upstairs to his bedroom for his packed bag, then to the curb. His final kiss held a passion that would only grow with distance.

I couldn't admit that I missed him already. We didn't

say such things out loud. It would be like admitting we were in a relationship. "Guess we're off again," I said.

He winked. "Until I get back."

I crossed my arms. "We'll see."

Twenty-one

Clothes are . . . nothing less than the furniture of the mind
made visible.   —JAMES LAVER

❧

Instead of sleeping, I dared to open Dom's closet and
study the contents from a distance with no intention of
touching anything wearable.

Unfortunately, the minute I did, I thought I heard
footsteps above me. But that would be somebody's bedroom, not the attic. Whew.

Just in case, though, I opened the cream, pink, and
mint green curtains and looked outside to see if those
bruised vines Nick pointed out were at this end of the
house.

Oh scrap, they were right here, one floor down, several curls of ivy having reached this very window. Why
couldn't I have noticed that before Nick left?

I stepped back to look for some kind of weapon to

keep near me and focused on the matching mosaic tables that Dom used for nightstands. They were round and unusual in antique white, inlaid with bits of Italian stained glass and old rose chinaware, with triple drawers, small, medium, and deep, and topped with small priceless mementos. Nothing I'd want to break over somebody's head in case of an emergency.

Was I letting my imagination run away with me? Did the wind offer a warning as it rattled the windows?

Now looking for clues and a weapon of sorts, I pulled down boxes from the closet shelves and looked through them.

I found love letters from several men, but one stack, clearly newer than the rest, had a note dated as recently as three weeks before and started with: "If you're nervous, dearest, please, go to the police." This guy spent a lot of time telling Dom why and how much he loved and adored her. The letter ended: "I can't wait to tell the world."

Tell the world about what?

The wind answered with a winter wail.

I looked for a return address on the torn envelope, but found none. Maybe they saw each other regularly. He signed his letters with an ornate V.

V. Victor? Pierce Pierpont's father was the only Victor, or V name, I'd heard since I got here.

I hoped it was Victor Pierpont and wondered if Pierce, who didn't seem fond of Dom, knew.

Gregor Zukovski was flaunted as Dominique's young

lover to the world while she might have had a more mature lover tucked away somewhere. Dom, you cheeky thing.

But Dom having Victor Pierpont as a lover was an assumption on my part. This V person, except for calling her "dearest" in the letter, could have been Dom's smitten paperboy for all I knew.

Right, and I was Nick's old prom date.

What exactly did this Victor know? I threw the letters on the bed, intending to read them in chronological order after I finished ransacking my friend's bedroom.

Nosing into her personal affairs was killing me. The need for a weapon was nearly as unnerving.

I looked out the window, again, this time toward the starry winter sky. "My apologies, my sweet friend. But you tagged me, and now I have to get nosy to follow through."

My cell phone rang. "Dolly, hello. Why are you up so late?"

"You know me," Dolly said. "I never sleep, and I've been sitting here trying to figure out who murdered your movie star friend."

I tried not to patronize her but encouraged the friendly speculation of an elderly neighbor who had always been there for four motherless Cutler kids. I mean nobody went to that many after-school events, from soccer to dorky plays without a great capacity for love or a gun to their heads. "Did you succeed in figuring it out?" I asked.

"I did," Dolly said. "It was Dominique DeLong's longtime rival. That rich ingénue biotch, Galina Lockhart, if you'll excuse my French."

Ah, Galina, Dom's rival in every way, according to Kyle. She who had noxious chemistry with Dom's ex. "And you came to that conclusion how, Dolly dear?"

"I'm a member of Dominique's fan club, and do you know that Galina dame keeps popping in?"

"Does she now? Where does she pop in?"

"On the computer chat page of the Dominique De-Long Fan Club, of course. Get with the times, cupcake. Join a dating service. Nick is just not getting off the stick."

Only because his stick is broken just now, I thought. "Dolly, back to Galina."

"Galina is saying outrageously sweet things about your friend as if she's lying to preserve Dom's memory, as if it *needs* preserving, like Dom deserved what she got." You know how gossip cats ace innuendo. They make the person they're saying something great about come out reeking. "Probably because the new star of *Diamond Sands* wants to smell sweet," Dolly conjectured incorrectly.

"Galina is not the new star of *Diamond Sands*. Ursula Uxbridge is."

"Oh," Dolly said. "Then why is Galina sniffing around Dominique's fan club?"

"Galina's an actress," I said, "Dom is dead. Ms. Lockhart always wants whatever Dom has, or had, in this case. Could she be angling for you and your friends to change your loyalty to her, bring you into the Galina Lockhart fan club?"

"Oh, that's too low to be believed," Dolly snapped.

Personally, I think Dolly called looking for details to share with Dom's fan club, but I didn't doubt that Galina—or more likely, her assistant—was nosing around pretending to be Dom's great and sad friend to cull a few fan club members for herself.

"I still think Galina did it," Dolly said, a little less certain. Really, you should tell the police. Promise."

"I'll tell." Nick. "Now try to get some sleep."

Dolly cleared her throat. "When's the funeral?"

There, that's what Dolly wanted to know. What a sly boots she was, so sharp for nearly a hundred and four years old.

"I'll have Eve email you when we get details." And I would too. Eve could email from her cell phone when we were on our way to the cemetery—since she'd asked about the funeral, not the wake—too late for a slew of fans to show up.

"Thanks and take care of yourself, cupcake."

"I will, sweetie. You, too."

"Night."

I clapped my phone shut and smiled. I'd needed a bit of normal. It was like Dom heard my prayer and sent me a kind heart to sustain me.

My guilt over Dom's death somewhat eased, I opened the deepest drawer at the bottom of the nightstand, probably on the side near which she slept, because it was closest to the bathroom. And what I saw in there left no doubt in my mind that Dom did, indeed, fear for her life.

I thought of Victor's words while I sorted through her munitions store. Why didn't she go to the police as he suggested? I found brass knuckles, a small handgun, loaded, a Barracuda stun gun, which I slipped in my pocket, advanced Taser, mace and pepper sprays, both tinted, and lipstick size, but one "stung wildfire hot." I also found a fogger and a mini alert alarm.

Every set of instructions was dog-eared; every item that needed a cartridge or batteries had freshly dated ones. Beside them were spares marked with future expiration dates.

All in all, Dom's arsenal spelled panic and the need to be prepared for anything.

Little good it had done her. She'd died of anaphylactic shock onstage in front of an audience without a chance to use one of her weapons.

I hadn't found anything like this at the theater, which made me look for her purse, and I remembered seeing it with the personal possessions that Kyle took home from the morgue today. She'd last carried a Gucci Hysteria bag in pewter, big enough for a small arsenal.

When I finished searching her room, I went into her bathroom, where I hung my dress on her door and washed my face. But while I was wiping it dry, I saw in the mirror that a drawer of the rattan lingerie chest had a Hermès scarf hanging from it, the vintage one I'd always lusted after.

I opened the drawer to set the scarf gently inside and found an exotic mauve satin peignoir set, a gorgeous display of 1980s lingerie, trimmed in ivory lace and satin rosebuds designed by Flora Nikrooz. Both pieces were freshly cleaned and tied with a lavender ribbon, a sprig of dried heather tucked in the bow.

From beneath the ribbon, I took a piece of Dom's stationery to read the note in her handwriting: *Mad Dearest, Wear us.*

Twenty-two

Judging by the ugly and repugnant things that are sometimes in vogue, it would seem as though fashion were desirous of exhibiting its power by getting us to adopt the most atrocious things for its sake alone. —GEORG SIMMEL

"What are you playing at, Dominique DeLong?" I called, looking around, as if I might see her ghost. "Are you starring as a puppeteer or casting me in the role of Alice in Wonderland? Because I'm feeling curiouser and curiouser."

I turned her note over to find a winking happy face.

"Damn. Do you expect this outfit to give me a vision?" God knew I'd already had more visions during this case than in any other of my experience, probably because of my heart connection to the deceased. God also knew how many more there'd be. I eyed the peignoir set and shivered. If Dom knew she was in danger, she'd been playing it for all it was worth and seemed to damn well revel in the game.

No. No one sets themselves up to die, least of all Dom with her joie de vivre, her zest for life. On the other hand, she'd been in show business for years and more than a bit jaded over the entertainment industry. Once a Broadway actress, she'd been knocked down a peg in the eyes of theater society when she accepted the leading role in an *off*-Broadway production.

I couldn't quite forget the vision I'd had of her in that crazy seventies room telling someone with a Frankenstein voice and wielding a Hula-hoop that it would be foolish for *them* to steal the diamonds.

I sighed, giving in to the inevitable, undressed, showered, and put on Dom's peignoir set, ambivalent about the vision it might, or might not, afford me. At this point, I needed to know every detail about Dominique's murder, whether I wanted to or not.

I had no sooner moved the Taser from my dress to the peignoir set pocket when a lethargic dizziness came over me, making my limbs feel heavy and not my own, the kind of warning that often presages a lengthy vision.

I hadn't made it to the bed when my cell phone rang.

I worked to fight the vision sucking me under as I answered, sounding a bit tipsy, even to my own ears.

"Go back to Connecticut or end up like your friend," my caller said through a voice modulator that made the speaker sound like some kind of robot werewolf.

I might be drunk on psychic energy, but I was smart enough to fear the threat more than the fake voice.

I hung up the phone in panic and turned so fast, I smacked my head against the open closet door and heard my phone hit the floor.

Not even the caller would expect me to get out of Dodge until tomorrow, so I didn't think the threat was immediate. Just as well because I needed badly to lie down.

Scrap it, I wished I was thinking more clearly.

I set a knee on the bed, my racing heart beginning to calm when my doorknob began to turn.

In danger of zoning into the vision seducing me, it occurred to me that the call might have been made from inside the house.

Unable to defend myself against a kitten, much less a killer, I slipped the Taser from my pocket and made my clumsy way to the door, needing to grab whatever I could to hold me up along the way.

I intended to lock the door, but it opened too fast, so I zapped the intruder—possibly the caller—with a knee-jerk move so swift and forceful, I surprised even me.

The twitching body hit the floor like a tree trunk, spasmed a couple more times, and stopped moving entirely. Out cold, or dead.

The possibility snapped me back from the edge like a faceful of ice water. I switched on the light. "Werner?"

I got down beside him and tapped his face. Failing to rouse him, I pried open an eyelid. "Are you in there? Please be alive."

He groaned but didn't wake. Whew.

I considered running but the vision in the peignoir set was still pulling me in, playing on my need to solve Dom's murder.

I got Werner on Dom's bed, though doing it sapped my fight against the black hole sucking me in.

He half helped as I got his torso, then finally both feet up there and I felt bad when I saw the bloody gash on his brow. He'd smacked his head on the floor, hard.

Now I couldn't fight the vision long enough to walk around the bed, so I crawled over him.

His moan reassured me as I dizzied my way into a different time and place, me sitting in this very room, in Dom's boudoir chair, the seafoam gown she'd sent me now in my lap, or in Dom's lap, actually.

She was wielding a pair of jewelry pliers to pry the pricey cubic zirconias from their settings, while deep inside myself, a fashion designer cringed.

Dom had taken on a tedious process. While I destroyed the gown, I noticed the empty bed with a different spread, blue curtains, and navy watered silk throw pillows. The lampshades now matched the pillows.

I worked quickly, almost in a panic, determined to get the gems from their settings, but why? All I knew was that my heart beat fast while I did, and my gaze kept straying to the door.

Then I saw the box of rhinestones beside me—rhinestones?—and wished I could ask questions. Like, why would I cheapen the dress? But I was alone. Scary alone, threatening shadows closing in on me.

No one from whom to seek help, no one to explain my task. Just "click, snap, click, snap."

In Dom's place, I was ruining the gown I had created.

Then the room tilted in jerky, uncoordinated movements, and the vision changed again.

I found myself in Dom's bed with a man. A great kisser. A wide-shouldered armful with an enviable amount of passion, hands everywhere, big hands, knowledgeable hungry lips, and an uber-talented tongue.

I wasn't sure if I was kissing one of Dom's lovers, or Ian, her ex-husband—ugh. Please don't let it be Ian.

I wanted to open my eyes, but they felt glued shut, as could only happen in dreams. No matter, I felt it best not to know the name of my dream-state lover.

Unfortunately turned on, I found it impossible not to return his enthusiasm, all our body parts meeting, dangerously well, ebbing and flowing, a coming together filled with depth and sizzle.

The phantom in my bed cupped my cheeks, held my face in place, made a meal of me, and whispered my name.

My name. Madeira. Not Dom or Dominique.

I woke, pulling from the kiss expecting to look straight into Nick's eyes.

Instead, I was looking into . . . Werner's?

I jumped from the bed as the door opened.

Eve stood for a minute like a doe in headlights, then she barked a laugh and added insult to injury by applauding. "Sinsational!" she snapped, her grin wide. "Can I tell Nick? Please, can I tell him? Can I, huh?"

"Has the world gone mad?" I asked, finding my bruise the hard way, by smacking it with the palm of my hand. "Ouch!"

"Madeira Cutler, you wicked girl." My erstwhile friend chuckled. "I've never been prouder."

Werner had never actually awakened. And I didn't know which made me wince more, the demented porker noises he was making or Eve's satisfaction in them.

"Do you mind?" I asked her as I sat on my side of the bed to clear my head.

"Not at all," Eve said, closing the door and coming closer to me, her grin making me want to erase it in a satisfying way.

Hands on her hips as she took in the sight of us, Eve shook her head. "Did you guys smoke a joint or something?"

"No, but I did have crazy dreams, that I'm now afraid might have been real, about zapping Tasers and a man shot down in his prime."

"Why do you have dry blood on your head? And Werner, too?" she asked. "You into something kinky? I was gonna ask if you were decent when I came in, but now I know the answer. You're engagingly and interestingly *indecent*, given that honeymoon-type negligee you're wearing."

"Stuff it Meyers."

"Too bad Sir Galahad is boringly, respectably dressed

beneath that blanket. Sheesh, what a downer. Way to burst a girl's bubble. There go all my fiendish hopes and dreams."

Eve rescued my cell phone from the floor. "What's Nick's speed-dial number?"

Twenty-three

Fashion is as profound and critical a part of the social life of man as sex, and is made up of the same ambivalent mixture of irresistible urges and inevitable taboos.   —RENÉ KÖNIG

Werner looked stoned as he woke with a snort and sat up like his hair was on fire. He also looked like he'd been beaten and left for dead.

Then there was his reaction to finding me in his bed. It was a mix of gladness, shock, and embarrassment.

Wooly knobby knits, were that man's pupils dilated or what? I might as well be a two-headed sasquatch the way he was looking at me.

His suit of gray pinstripes, now a wrinkled shambles, gave him the look of a homeless off-duty detective. Given the confusion written on his bloody brow, his brain appeared to be working in the way his suit fit, both him and it, off the rack, barely on a hanger, aka hanging by a thread.

The way he regarded Eve and I, he didn't know his own name, never mind ours.

"What I wouldn't give to have planted a camera in this room last night," Eve said, laughing like she'd been chasing a rainbow and caught it. "Seriously, where's the fed? Did you trade him in, finally? Thank God."

"Can it," Werner and I said, both with a wince because of our bruises.

He scrubbed his face with both hands, sighed, and looked at me. "Please tell me that we did *not* sleep together."

"We did *not* sleep together," I said, trying to convince myself while examining the robe of the peignoir set. Two diaphanous layers did not a covering make. Afraid to grab a wrap or coat from Dom's closet, lest I be given an unwanted vision, I chose a crocheted throw, made of roses in pinks and greens, from the foot of the bed and used it as a shawl. There, now I felt more in charge.

Werner gazed up and down my body, looking rather affronted.

"Well," I said, "your pupils may be dilated, but your eyes can still twinkle."

"You're *sure* we didn't sleep together?" he asked.

"You so did." Eve, the Cheshire Cat, sat at the foot of the bed, her back against the footboard, ankles crossed, as if she were settling in for a juicy chat.

"We apparently slept in the same bed," I said, mostly to myself, "but I have no memory of how we got there. Werner? Do you?"

He opened his hands, regarded his palms, and his eye twinkle returned. "I have *tactile* memories."

I resented the traitorous thrill that skittered up my spine. Oh goodie. Not.

"Give that man a lottery ticket," Eve said. "It's his lucky day."

I closed the crocheted throw tighter over my breasts as I paced, until I saw the crack in my cell phone, which bothered me, a lot.

Werner raised himself on an elbow. "Mad, Madeira, did I, I mean, did we . . . ?"

"He means," Eve said, tongue in cheek. "Was it as good for you as it was for him?"

"Eve, you're not helping at all," I said, taking pity on Werner. "I wish I could remember." Broken cell phone case—stepped on, thrown, dropped?

"Let's just forget whatever it was that happened," Werner said, as if that could be the end of it.

Eve rose to the occasion. "Unless Mad got pregnant."

Werner and I whipped our gazes her way like we were fine brass gears moving as one, hungry attack gears, and Eve was dinner.

"Not funny, Meyers," I said, but that didn't mean my heart wasn't playing jump rope. *Hippity hickety hop; How many months before I pop? Cinderella slept with a fella, made a mistake and kissed a snake; How many doctors did it take?*

Ack, even an old jump-rope rhyme was working

127

against me. "I just wish I could *remember* what happened," I muttered.

Eve raised a brow. "Whose nightgown are you wearing?"

"I don't even care," Werner said. "I'm just so glad she's wearing it."

"Because it's see-through?" Eve asked.

"Because she's not naked," Werner snapped.

I sighed. "It's *Dom's* peignoir set," I said, giving Eve a wide-eyed stare so she'd "get a clue" that I zoned. "It had my name on it, like the seafoam gown." Hint, hint.

"Ohhhh," Eve said, *getting* it, then grinning like a loon. "The plot thickens. You really *don't* know what happened here last night. Intrigue can be so much fun."

I sat on the edge of the bed to face the man who'd slept beside me, the thought making me think of Nick, which raised guilt like bile inside me. Mind games powered by panic, I thought.

"Lytton, tell us why you're here in New York, then we'll talk about why you're in my bed."

He rubbed his face, a nervous habit, with another wince and another ouch for his bloody bruised brow, and he sighed in resignation. "Nick's house alarm went off right after dark, yesterday, and again at seven twenty, so I had a chance to talk to him on the phone a couple of times. He thinks somebody's after that dress you designed, and they could just as easily be after you."

"Scrap, I hope Dom's gown is safe at his place."

"I've got a detail watching the house," Werner said,

"but after Nick expressed his regret that he wasn't here to keep an eye on you, I got to thinking that by coming here, I could maybe solve the attempted break-ins. If they are related to that dress, there is a good chance the intruder knew Dominique and will be at the funeral. *And* I can watch your back."

My spine stiffened without conscious thought on my part. "Did Nick ask you to keep an eye on me?"

Eve snorted. "If he did, can I call him and tell him what a knock-up job, er, I mean a bang-up job, Werner's doing? Pretty please?"

Twenty-four

Vain trifles as they seem, clothes . . . change our view of the world, and the world's view of us. —VIRGINIA WOOLF

❧

"The dry blood on both your foreheads might be a clue as to why you can't remember much," Eve pointed out. "And why was your cell phone on the floor? It's cracked, you know."

"It was on the floor?" I asked, a niggling memory trying to resurface.

"Yes, did something besides Werner frighten you last night?"

The phone call came to me in a rush. "Someone called and told me in an altered voice to go back to Connecticut or end up like my friend."

Werner frowned. "Then what?"

"I dropped the phone, and turned so fast, I walked into the open closet door." I touched my poor bruised forehead.

Eve's eyes narrowed. "Were you wearing the peignoir set at the time?"

I nodded, aware that I hadn't been quite myself.

Werner looked at Eve like she was nuts. "I know clothes are important to you two, but I'm guessing there's no proper attire for when your life is threatened."

Eve giggled while Werner came around the bed and touched my temple, so gently, I saw my pain reflected in his gaze, and I found it necessary to pull away so as not to be pulled toward . . . something.

The gash across his brow looked deeper than mine, as if he'd been hit at close range. I stroked it as gently as he'd touched mine.

He jumped like I burned him.

"Did someone conk us both on the head?" I wondered aloud. "I suppose an intruder could have tried to climb up to the window. The vines are thick enough to hold a man. Nick said they were scraped like they'd been climbed. He had the police check them out."

"Why would anybody want to hurt you?" Werner asked.

I gave a half shrug because a whole shrug would have hurt my head. "Beats the spinning slubs out of me."

Someone knocked on the hall door, and Werner scooted into the bathroom.

I closed the door behind him.

Eve let in Kerri, Dom's maid, bearing a pushcart topped with a silver coffee service, two cups, linen napkins, and a plate of croissants.

"Thank you, Kerri," I said. "You're a godsend."

Kerri bobbed, an interrupted curtsey, since I'd asked her not to. "Did your man find your room all right?"

"My man?" I asked.

"I let him in late last night and when he mentioned working with you, I directed him to this room."

"Yes, yes, he found me."

Eve poured a cup of coffee and handed it to me.

"All clear, Werner," I called through the door, though I needn't have bothered.

"I know," he said coming out. "I heard."

I gave him my cup of coffee.

His look of gratitude overshadowed the deed.

I swiped Eve's coffee from her hand, took a sip, and handed it back.

"Hey," she snapped, but something caught her eye and dissipated her affront. "Is that a Taser on the floor?"

Werner groaned and for the first time, he looked like the mad Wiener. "Madeira Cutler, you Tasered me!"

"You don't know that for sure." But I was beginning to remember things. I saw Dom's drawer of evil weapons, open a crack, so I backed up to the bed and unobtrusively pushed the drawer shut with the back of my leg.

The damned thing squealed closed.

Werner set his cup on the dresser, took me by the arms, set me aside, and opened the drawer. "Your arsenal?"

"Dominique's, dammit."

Eve took a look and whistled. "She must really have been afraid. I think she knew her life was in danger."

"It looks that way," Werner said, eyeing me.

"I didn't know you were coming," I said. "I was in my dead friend's bedroom and I'd just found . . . that!" I indicated the weapons. "You'd have nightmares, too, if you'd identified her body then got threatened with the same fate." To my utter horror, I started to cry.

I had never seen Werner look panicked before. He took me in his arms and rocked me while he patted my back. "I'm sorry, Mad. I didn't know you'd identified the body. Couple that with the threat, the discovery of a torture drawer, and I can see why you'd have been spooked."

Eve raised a brow as she watched us, but she said nothing.

"Did you get Tasered, too?" Werner asked me. "That might make you forget."

So might zoning into reading a vintage outfit, I thought, but what did I get out of it? Nothing. I had no recollection of the— Wait. Yes I did. I saw Dom switching my pricey cubic zirconias for cheap old rhinestones on the seafoam gown somebody was now trying to steal from Nick's house.

Eve picked up the Taser.

"What I can't figure out," Werner said, taking it cautiously from Eve's hand and setting it gently in Dom's arsenal, "is why somebody doesn't want you at your friend's funeral."

Before I could warn Eve with a look, she shrugged. "Simple," she said. "Mad's making somebody nervous with her investigation."

Werner turned on me. "Madeira Cutler, are you sleuthing again?"

Twenty-five

As long as you know men are like children, you know everything!
—COCO CHANEL

❧

"I'm a sleuth," I admitted. "So arrest me."

Werner sighed. "Cute. Did you get the phone call before or after you found Dom's ghoulish stash?"

"I found the stash first, and it scared the bejeebers out of me."

Werner squeezed my arm. "You were already skittish when your life was threatened then. No wonder you panicked."

"So you forgive me for Tasering you? Because I remember now that I did."

"I don't suppose I have a choice."

"Good, then see if you can forgive me for this." I opened my purse, took out the note I got from Dom with the dress, and handed it to Werner. "Here. It was taped between the tissue around Dom's dress the other morning."

He scanned it, then tapped it against the palm of his hand for a long minute. "In a way, your friend practically asked you to sleuth. Why didn't you tell me?"

"It wasn't your jurisdiction?"

His nod held a grudging respect. "The caliber of your pretexts are improving. Good one."

I smiled for the first time that day. "Thank you."

"What does she mean by special talents?" he asked. "Are you supposed to *design* an answer?"

"Mad's intuitive," Eve said. "Dominique knew that."

I mentally thanked Eve for her great answer.

"So intuitive," Werner said, "that you don't know whether you cheated on Jaconetti last night or not?"

"That's low," I said, "even for you."

"Yes," Werner agreed. "It was low. I'm feeling the sting of you keeping that note from me. I apologize. If anything happened last night, it would *have* to have happened under the influence of our double concussive head traumas. I mean, we'd both be smarter than that in our right minds."

"Right." Why didn't I like his tone? "What?" I snapped. "Am I not good enough for you?"

Eve's laughter bubbled forth. "Mad, quit while you're ahead and all that?"

"Right. Listen, Lytton. I did Taser you after, but first I saw the torture devices, heard steps above me, got a death threat, smacked my head, then somebody turns my doorknob and comes in. Of course my instinct was to zap. I'm just sorry it was you."

"If it had been anybody else, I'd applaud your instincts." He sounded resigned.

"Kind of makes my previous unintentional attacks pale in comparison, doesn't it?" I said.

"Pale yes. A pale blue, because that's the color this bruise is gonna be, blue like my old friend, the mace you carry." He smiled at the reference to one of my past accidental attacks on him.

"Wait till Nick sees your matching bruises," Eve said, "and hears about last night. Where is Nick, by the way?"

"Off on assignment chasing the Pierpont diamonds halfway across the world," I said. "Where's Kyle?"

"Kyle's calling for the limo. The wake starts in—" She looked at her watch. "Oops, half an hour."

"Ack!" I jumped from the bed. I'd been so busy searching for clues in Dom's room last night that I forgot to unpack. "I need to get my dress steamed."

When I put my bag on the bed and opened it, however, I found Nick's clothes, instead of my own. "I knew that getting matching luggage was a stupid idea." We'd been at the mall and the sale was too good to pass up for either of us. Black Tumi Alpha luggage. Figures any time we did something that smacked of being a couple it backfired! I shook my head. "Thank God I keep my makeup in my purse."

"Nick's gonna look hot in vintage Versace," Eve muttered. "I'll tell Kyle to hold the limo for an extra half hour," she said. "They won't start without him."

Werner picked up both his garment and overnight bags. "I'm going to take a shower and get dressed."

"Uh, can I have a minute in there first?"

"Oh, sure."

"Why are you here, again, exactly?" I asked before going into the bathroom.

"Besides seeing if Nick's attempted housebreaks are related, I'd say it's to keep you out of trouble, and to keep people safe from your Taser-happy trigger finger. And Nick did hint that you might need someone."

I slammed the bathroom door in Werner's face. "I'll beat you both later," I yelled.

When I came out, Werner disappeared into the bathroom for his shower.

Dom's everyday closet was still open from the night before. I looked at the outfits lined up there, shook my head, and opened her walk-in closet of vintage clothes, actually an adjoining bedroom that had been converted.

In the chill air of the climate-controlled room, I picked out the dress that had been Coco Chanel's personal little black dress, the one she wore herself when she was photographed in 1936 by Man Ray. It was practically the crown jewel of Dom's vintage collection, and since I was prepared to buy it—having first pick and all—I felt safe wearing it.

I know I'd teased Dom about my wearing this dress and reading Coco, but it was the only dress I could be sure *not* to read Dom herself in, because she'd once told me it was too precious to wear. As for reading Coco, it wasn't likely. Aunt Fiona, our very own Mystick Falls witch, had told me that my gift was a mandate from the universe. Simply put, clothes that spoke to me did so for a reason, usually in reference to an event that shot negative energy into the universe like fireworks begging metaphysical assistance. Enter the psychic daughter of a psychic witch—*moi*!

I'd be safe from my visions in this.

A simple round-necked, long-sleeved shirtwaist, this historically exciting little black dress had a four-inch neck slit that tied together at the center top with a bow.

With its mid-calf hem, it was perfect for a funeral. I paired it with a jaunty Chanel hat from Coco's very early days in France, its curled feather placed to cover the gash on my head. To go with them, I chose 1995 black suede Louboutin pumps trimmed in grosgrain ribbon, its heels designed after the curves of a woman's body. I topped the outfit with Dom's multistrand pearls.

I was glad I'd showered late the night before, because we were short on time and my hair always looked better on the second day. I used the chilly dressing room to get dressed in, then I sat at Dom's dressing table to put on my makeup.

When Werner came out of the bathroom, he whistled.

I took the compliment as my due or actually as owing to my fashion sense. "You don't look half bad, yourself," I said. "Navy pinstripes suit you."

He fingered the feather on my hat, and I believe that we both realized, in that moment, the magnitude of our having slept together—well, slept in the same bed at any rate—I remembered the last place his hand had rested, and I tingled there.

For his part, he flexed and fisted that same hand.

Why had we tuned in to that together? Why did our gazes hold and linger while my temperature rose and the February wind outside the window seemed like a serenade?

I shook away my lethargy and looked in the mirror. "Dom's clothes, her perfume, her jewelry. Why do I get the feeling she engineered this?"

Werner straightened his cuffs. "Are you saying I was part of the plan?"

"You're never part of the plan, Werner, but you always end up being a critical part of the action."

"Is that a compliment?"

"No. It's the reason I should be afraid of you."

Twenty-six

Black is the color most often chosen to cloak the pious and those devoted to spiritual sacrifice. The flip side of black suggests a darker nature . . . calling up references to mystery, magic, and inevitably, a little bit of sin.
—AMY HOLMAN EDELMAN, *THE LITTLE BLACK DRESS*

My dear friend was dead, sealed in a horrendously expensive bronze coffin, according to Kyle, that *should* be sitting on the empty pedestal at the head of the room.

Behind the pedestal hung a life-sized picture of Dominique, at her most glamorous, the one in which she'd posed for the cover of *Vogue* wearing Christian Dior.

On the wall beside it hung a picture nearly as glamorous, but so full of life, you expected Dom to step right out of it and hug you. I felt both honored and humbled to be in that candid with her and her son at the skating rink at Rockefeller Center, taken more than a year ago.

"I shouldn't be in that picture," I told Kyle. "You should have picked one with just you and your mom."

"Give it up, Mad. She thought of you as a friend and

daughter. I started calling you Aunt Mad because I was jealous as a kid, but I saw the error of my ways the minute I asked for your help after she passed, and you came, no questions asked."

"I'm honored. Sincerely."

"Yesterday at the train station, I saw in you what Mom saw from the beginning," Kyle said. "A kindred spirit, a kind soul. Family. From now on, can I just call you Sis?"

Okay, I thought, he must be sedated. "Of course."

"What will you call me?" Eve asked him in a whisper to tease the sadness from his expression.

"Nothing that I can repeat in polite company," he said, nuzzling her ear and pulling her close against his side. She had become his weapon against despair. Hardly the stuff of a lasting relationship, but I figured Eve knew that.

Without Nick, I felt lost, and beside Kyle and Eve, a fifth wheel. Ian, Kyle's ex-dad, must have seen my discomfort and decided to take me in hand, because he stepped up to take my arm.

Attached to him, I felt like I needed a hazmat chemical wash. Ugh. I extricated myself from the man who hurt my friend and made a beeline for Werner. "I don't belong here in the inner circle," I said.

He cleared his throat and turned me toward the skating rink picture. "She really was your friend," he said. "I'm sorry I didn't get it the other morning."

"What are you really doing here? I mean, thank you,

but aren't you afraid that Mystick Falls will fall apart without you?"

"Nah, I had some vacation time coming, and I was just looking for a good excuse when somebody got interested in Nick's house."

"You were worried about me."

"Life gets interesting around you, Mad, and dangerous. Very dangerous."

I may have been ticked, but when he took my arm as Pierce Pierpont approached, turning the unlikable man in another direction, I was relieved to belong to someone. Well, paired off, anyway. I didn't belong to Werner.

Werner enforced the law while coloring within the lines. Me, there wasn't a line I hadn't crossed with crayons, or otherwise, my whole life, except for maybe the law, most of the time. I did *try* not to break that.

The silence between us became uncomfortable. "What's taking so long?" I wondered out loud.

"The police are downstairs going through Dominique's casket," Werner said.

"On the day of the funeral? That's odd," I said. "How do you know that?"

"I'm a law enforcement officer. I made it a point to introduce myself as a friend of the family, offer my services, if necessary, and tell them I'd stay out of their way, otherwise."

"As a courtesy then?"

"And to find out what was happening."

"So you could keep me apprised?"

"You, I'm going to keep out of trouble."

I stepped away and huffed.

"Per Eve's request," Werner said, "I'm also supposed to protect you from the worms in the Big Apple."

"Oh, for heaven's sakes, there are worms everywhere, even in Mystic. Haven't we proved that?" But I looked back at the empty stand for the casket and shivered.

"Are you cold? Do you want me to have them turn down the air-conditioning?" Werner suddenly looked like the protective, sensitive guy who'd once saved me from a fire and carried me home in the middle of the night.

Twenty-seven

It is as if each of us has one titular robe, and it is that special black dress that is both chic and armor.
—EDNA O'BRIEN, *MIRABELLA*

Restless, in the lush foyer parlor, Broadway and Hollywood greats were milling about waiting for a nod to file in beside the missing coffin. In other words, they wanted to pay their respects to Dominique. Never mind that some of them, not all by any means, didn't know the meaning of the word "respect."

A few I had designed clothes for under Faline's label during my years here in the New York fashion industry. There were several greats, who, under less serious circumstances, I might be tempted to fan-slobber over.

Thank the occasion for dignity.

There were also designer mourners, with ruthlessly cold blood, who I already suspected could have murdered Dom.

"Who do you think killed her?" Werner asked, suddenly beside me.

"Have you been reading my mind?"

"Mind reading. I thought that was your territory."

"What?" What the hell did he know? I'd definitely never mentioned my visions to Werner. He already thought I was a scatterbrain. I didn't want him to question my sanity.

"You said you were here because Ms. DeLong trusted your *intuitive* instincts."

Oh. Whew. "Okay, here are my prime suspects so far, because they all had means, motive, and opportunity," I whispered. "At first look, Ursula Uxbridge, understudy, who got Dom's starring role in *Diamond Sands*. The morning papers said she was a hit last night, better than Dom, the best ever to play the role, sad to say. Though I'm not sure she has the smarts.

"Second suspect, Ian DeLong, ex-husband, ex-dad, brilliant, if greedy, business partner, who will probably inherit the other half of Dom's business interests because of the sheer genius partnership contract that couldn't be broken, even in the divorce.

"Three, Zander Pollock, world-class private chef. Dom died from a lethal dose of peanuts, and that allergy is why she hired Pollock in the first place. She couldn't smell a peanut without her throat tightening."

"The chef is too obvious," Werner said.

"Gee, thanks."

"I hate to tell you, but so's the ex and the understudy. Got anybody else?"

"Shudup!"

Werner shook his head and walked away.

I peeked into the waiting area, again. Dominique had friends in high places who thought that being seen at her wake and memorial service would help their careers. Or they might meet someone here who could.

The outfit of the day was the little black dress; the subject of much fashion study, primarily credited to Coco Chanel, and was responsible for my fashion nook, Little Black Dress Lane, a very busy place in my shop.

While Kyle talked to the funeral director about the missing casket, Eve stood on tiptoe behind me, peeking into the luxurious cream, gold, and blue foyer waiting room at the stars gathered there. "Hey, Mad, I see a dress that says, 'Take me, big boy.'"

"What?" I asked, craning my neck. "Mae West is here?"

Eve gave me a raised brow.

I shrugged. "I'm just saying."

She returned to her gawking.

"Eve, that angry woman in the scanty black Oscar de la Renta looks familiar. Do you remember who she is?"

"Angry woman?" Kyle asked. Now behind us, he stood a head taller and had a clearer view. "Oh, that's Galina Lockhart, remember? Mom's primary rival. Galina's dress and stance say she's pissed at being kept waiting. She's also jealous that Mom is in here and she's not."

"Huh?" Eve said. "She wants to be dead?"

"No, Galina has always simply wanted to be more important than my mother in any situation, and if she doesn't get her way, move over or she'll mow you down."

Twenty-eight

The consciousness of being perfectly dressed may bestow a peace such as religion cannot give.   —HERBERT SPENCER

As Eve moved away, I saw two people coming through the celebrity throng who warmed my heart. "Dad?" I called. "Aunt Fiona?"

They saw me, headed my way, and I let them in, ignoring the grumbles from the people I closed out.

"Dad," I said, my eyes welling up. "I've never been happier to see anyone in my life."

Kyle turned away, but I caught his arm. "Kyle, I want you to meet my parents."

My father paled.

"I mean, this is my dad, Professor Harry Cutler."

"Professor," Kyle said, shaking his hand. "Your daughter's a marvel."

My dad preened just a bit. "I know."

I hooked my arm through Aunt Fee's. "And this is my aunt Fiona."

"We're not married," my father rushed to say, "or related . . . or anything."

Aunt Fiona elbowed him.

"Aunt Fee is a family friend who was there for us after my mother passed. I was ten. She's not one of my parents, strictly speaking."

"Well, Aunt Fee, if I may," Kyle said. "It seems to me that Mad and her siblings were lucky to have had you."

"We still are," I said, "lucky to have her. Aren't we, Dad?"

Dad the Professor cleared his throat. " 'One never can tell from the sidewalk just what the view is to someone on the inside, looking out.' That's a quote by George Ade from *Knocking the Neighbors*, and it's particularly salient to this disconcerting turn in the conversation."

Aunt Fiona patted his arm. "Well said, dear."

"Oh no. You called him 'dear' in public. Aunt Fee. He may need smelling salts."

My father blustered but not for long. " 'How sharper than a serpent's tooth it is to have a thankless child!' "

"Shakespeare, we know," Aunt Fiona whispered.

I chuckled, and so did Kyle as he excused himself and walked away.

"Dad? Do you need to lie down?"

"Stop it," he snapped. "Both of you."

I thought we'd better heed his warning. "So, Aunt Fiona," I said hugging her. "Who's watching the shop?"

I could feel her squaring her shoulders beneath my embrace. "Now, we're only staying for the day, so don't worry, but Olga Meyers, and Ethel and Dolly Sweet are at the shop, with Tunney Lague on call in case of an emergency."

Eve hooted. "My mother'll clean and make sure all the customers are happy, and if she can figure out how, she'll feed them, too."

"And Ethel, the cranky octogenarian, will complain," Werner said.

I chuckled. "While our Dolly, allowed at a hundred and three years old, will lounge on the fainting couch and issue orders." But I knew better. Dolly would also flirt with Dante, my hunky ghost and her one-time lover. No secret, there. Dante Underhill, undertaker, left her his fortune with the funeral carriage house, the building she more or less gave to me for my shop—for the price of taxes.

"Sounds like everything back home is in good hands," I said.

Did you see that crowd out there?" my father asked. "They're half naked at a funeral. 'Never in the history of fashion has so little material been raised so high to reveal so much that needs to be covered so badly,' " he quoted. "Cecil Beaton," he said, giving due credit.

"Quite the who's who of celebrity land," Aunt Fiona said. "I feel positively nobody."

By then the funeral directors were coming in and herding our little circle into a small anteroom so they could set the casket in place.

This made my heart race. Seeing Dom in her coffin would make it real.

I didn't want it to be real.

My father and Aunt Fiona flanked me, as if to protect me, as we made our way to the small parlor.

"What took so long?" I asked Kyle when he joined us.

"The police were tearing up her coffin lining, looking for the diamonds, and I refused to send her to her eternal reward in torn satin."

"She would never have forgiven you if you tried," I said.

"Right, so I had her put in a fresh coffin. It took a good argument and a lot of time."

"Why did the police wait until she was inside the coffin?"

"They thought the fact that we were burying her so fast with no announcement at all was suspicious—they just didn't get me trying to avoid ten thousand fans parading through—and they figured the placement of her body would indicate which coffin needed to be searched."

"Like she was gonna take the diamonds with her?"

"No," Kyle said. "Like her murderer was going to dig her up later and retrieve the diamonds."

"Gross."

Kyle straightened his tie. "Tell me about it."

Werner rocked on his heels. "I've seen it done. Caught the murderer digging the old lady up. Casket's memento drawer full of stolen jewelry."

Every one of us looked his way.

He simply shrugged.

Finally, when they let us into the room with Dom, the casket was open, temporarily. We alone were being allowed to view the body before they closed it for her wake and memorial service.

Though she did look fine in that strapless black vintage Atelier Versace gown, with just a sprinkling of Pierpont diamonds, no amount of makeup could have fixed her face to her satisfaction, or mine.

"They made her look beautiful," I whispered to Kyle as I took the kneeler and he stood looking down at her. It wasn't true, of course. Her face looked ghastly, even covered in makeup. I wept despite myself.

In the middle of my tears, a sickness swept over me. A miasma of floaty nausea. Oh no, I thought. I can't pass out now. It would be so embarrassing. I bowed my head, so it would look like I was praying while I let the dizziness pass.

When my light-headedness abated, I raised my head, but Dominique no longer lay in the casket before me, this one a copper casket, not bronze, had a blue lining, not cream.

Inside, a handsome, mature man with a head of dark hair, a bit white at the temples, wore a Nehru jacket— weird even when it was popular—and a manly diamond as big as my fist.

My heart broke just to look at him.

I wondered how long ago he died, but someone

stopped with a memorial program and I saw that it was dated only two weeks before.

Dom had just lost someone she cared deeply for, a gorgeous man a bit older than her, though she reportedly had a young lover: Gregor Zukovski, possible Slavic diamond smuggler.

I realized that I was patting the dead man's clasped hands, while mine were swathed in black lace Victorian gloves, circa 1860, and I was sobbing, heartbroken, over his loss.

In this state between psychic awareness and reality, I sometimes lost myself. Now I wanted to know if my gut-wrenching tears were for Dom or for her lover.

Of course! I *wasn't* myself, anymore, I was Dom. But I was feeling Dom's feelings. Either my psychometric ability had been kicked up a notch from use, or wearing a dear friend's clothes made the vision stronger.

Previous to this, I would be a casual observer in someone else's clothes, but right now I was experiencing a range of emotions, not the least of which was a debilitating grief.

I'd zoned and was having a vision and a half. Wow, hard to get a clue when you're grieving for two people at the same time.

Scrap. I knew Dominique would only have worn Coco's extraordinary and valuable dress to a very special event. Obviously this man meant the world to her.

Was this Deep Throat? I wondered. If so, they never did get to run away together.

"I'm so sorry about your dad," I heard from a man in my line of vision talking to the family.

"Victor was a good man," said the next to pay her respects. "The best."

Pierce Pierpont wearing a black Canali suit and diamond studs in his French-cuffed white silk shirt stood accepting condolences from a long line of people.

The man Dom had loved *was* Pierpont's father. And he had passed away only two weeks before.

Kyle had said that Pierpont sent her flowers before every performance. Not Pierce but Victor, who simply signed them Pierpont.

Son of a stitch, I thought, as my vision hazed and I began floating dangerously away, I had to find out what Victor Pierpont died of.

Twenty-nine

Guilt is perhaps the most painful companion of death.
—COCO CHANEL

"I hate smelling salts," I said as I coughed and turned from the stench, feeling more myself again, embarrassed to realize that I was on the floor flat on my back at eye level with the base of the kneeler and casket stand, my dad and Werner, among others, bending over me.

"What happened?" I asked, as if I didn't know, though I'd only passed out during a psychometric vision before. Then again, I'd only talked that one time, too. Which meant that I never knew what to expect.

"You fainted," my father said, while Werner helped me up. He attempted to walk me to a chair, but I turned back to the coffin, because I needed to see Dominique one more time.

Werner nodded and moved away.

I went to the casket and patted her hands the way she patted Victor Pierpont's. I'll find out what happened to *both* of you, I promised, though I wondered why I found the old man's death suspicious at all.

Oh yeah, I remember. I'd been kneeling in Dom's place. *She* had been suspicious.

I heard Kyle's voice rise as he spoke with the funeral director. Kyle insisted on closing the lid himself, well, "ourselves," he said.

"It just isn't done," the director argued.

Kyle stepped up to the man, close and threatening. Not Kyle's style at all, or was it?

Then again, grief is a mighty stressor that can cause exacerbated reactions.

"For a hundred-and-fifty-thousand-dollar funeral," Kyle whispered furiously, "I would hope that an exception could be made, because if it can't, people will want to know." This made Kyle's words the kind of threat that metaphorically raised the funeral director in the air by his shirt collar.

"Of course, Mr. DeLong," the director said, backing away and smoothing the metaphorical wrinkles in his suit.

Kyle came up beside me, kissed his mother's cheek, and asked if I was ready. When I nodded, we slowly lowered the lid on Dom's casket.

With my heart in my throat, it was among the most difficult things I'd ever had to do, and yet, I knew it was what Dom would have wanted.

I would never forget my last view of her dear face. I tried to see her radiant beauty, instead of her ravaged features, while I swallowed convulsively.

When we finished, Kyle and I looked at the picture of us together. That was the memory I'd rather take with me.

Startling everyone, the sound of Dominique singing "Amazing Grace" filled the room blanketing it in shocked silence, except for her extraordinary voice.

I went to sit beside Dad, who was holding Aunt Fiona in his arms, her face against his chest.

Of course this would be hard for Aunt Fee. She'd had a casket trauma of her own to deal with, like being shut inside one not that long ago.

Werner handed me the cup of water he'd been holding. "Are you all right?" he whispered. "That was brave."

"What, passing out?"

"No, closing the lid."

My hand shook as I sipped the water, and that's when it hit me that I wouldn't see Dom ever again.

Aunt Fiona gave me a tissue.

My dad put his other arm around me and gave me his spare shoulder, sturdy and familiar. That's why they'd come. To be here for me.

Up front, Kyle took his place to receive the world's sympathy and with a raised brow, he turned his ex-dad away from the family receiving line.

Ian looked like he'd won some kind of game as he came to sit in the front row with us, even though he should be ashamed of losing his son's respect and having it witnessed by all of us.

To my surprise, after "Amazing Grace," Dominique's vocals continued with the songs she sang in *Diamond Sands* and some she didn't sing in the show: "Diamonds Are a Girl's Best Friend," "Lucy in the Sky with Diamonds," "This Diamond Ring," "Diamond Girl," "Diamonds in the Mine," "Diamonds and Guns," and more were piped softly into the room. They may not all have been used in the show but diamonds were the common theme.

Was that a clue? Dom kept an arsenal. She had somehow shipped me the dress saying if I had it, she was dead. Had she also planned her funeral, songs and all? I'd have to ask Kyle. I couldn't leave any possibility, however remote, unchecked.

Kyle stood alone and received New York's elite with his head high and Galina Lockhart first in line. Dom's well-chronicled rival did not look like she enjoyed Dom's vocal supremacy while *she* was trying to talk, and that made her steam.

It made me smile.

Eve and I were too close to the line of mourners to comment on the clothes, a hobby of ours, but I watched the face of every person who entered the room, and I made notes as to how they reacted when they saw the casket.

Sometimes Dad or Fiona supplied the name of a celebrity from their generation. Werner told me the names of a couple of gorgeous starlets, "hot and upcoming," he said, but I didn't recognize them.

After the service, the funeral director stood to make an announcement. "The interment, immediately following the service, will be private, but you're all invited to a funeral collation at the Pierpont Mansion at four this afternoon."

In the stretch Lamborghini, I called Dolly to tell her we were on our way to the funeral, as promised. The trip to the cemetery seemed more bizarre than anything so far today, though it might rival yesterday.

The unnamed mausoleum looked like what I perceived heaven should, especially if you were Dominique. I wouldn't be surprised if she oversaw its design.

Constructed of carved white marble outside, the inside mixed the white with a claret marble, and an allover pale pink marble, predominant in the handkerchief-skirted angels with flowing hair, offering a rose in each hand.

For the occasion, bouquets of multicolored roses stood on towering stands and filled every corner of Dom's place of eternal rest. Knowing Kyle, they might continue to do so.

I was overwhelmed by both the beauty of this place and by my grief.

The design and palette struck an overall mood: hard marble carved to a soft beauty, cold to the touch but warm to the spirit, beautiful, peaceful, comfortable.

A haven for eternity.

As we stood surrounding the casket, a woman entered wearing flowing white robes, dragonfly jewelry, and carrying a crystal wand. Then I recognized the table at the foot of the casket for what it was, an altar. On it, ritual candles, cup, knife, lavender oil, crystals, a pentacle, incense, a bell . . . Wiccan tools all.

Dom told me years ago that she was Wiccan. Back then, I didn't know that my mother had also been a practicing witch.

"My name," the white-robed woman said, "is Danica, and I'm a high priestess. Dominique asked me to perform a ritual to bring you comfort and send her to the Summerland, the Elysian Fields, or to a place where you would rather think of her as being peaceful and happy. I invite any witches here present to step up and take part in seeing Dominique on a wondrous and joyous journey."

Danica cast the circle and after a bit of hesitation, Aunt Fiona stepped up to work beside her. My father and I turned to look at each other as the light scent of chocolate wafted by us. My mother urging me to take part in sending Dom on her way. For my friend, I thought.

After a nod from my father, I took my place beside Aunt Fiona. I had loved Dominique and she deserved my participation.

My father's expression turned inward, and he seemed neither judgmental nor approving. Good progress, Dad.

Danica set a piece of smoking white sage in a silver dragonfly burner, and lit a tapered fireplace match. "I light this candle to celebrate the life of Dominique

DeLong. Recall your favorite memory of her. Your best memories are the ones she wants to take with her, and by recalling them, you will be sending them to her."

"The pink candle is for love, the blue for peace. She wishes to leave you with both. The white candle will protect you from grief. Visualize Dominique beside you. Hug her and say goodbye so she can leave. Imagine her stepping into the light, greeting loved ones who have gone before, resting in glory for as long as she pleases, then reincarnating and returning to you."

Kyle smiled. I found suddenly that I could, too.

For a short service, Danica's ritual packed a wallop, and peace filled me as we left the mausoleum. Aunt Fee put her arm around my waist as we stood with my dad beside the casket. "I smell chocolate," Aunt Fee said. "Your mom is with us."

"Yes. She reminded me to take my place at the altar, for Dominique's sake."

Dad cleared his throat and took off his glasses to clean them. Perhaps he felt my mother's presence more keenly than either of us.

Thirty

I think fashion is that we go two steps forward and go fifteen back each time because you always have to look back and see what's been done.
—BOB MACKIE

※

After everyone left the DeLong mausoleum, Kyle leading the way, I stood beside the casket for a minute alone with Dom. "I'll find out who did this to you. I promise."

When I got outside, people were still milling about as if they didn't want to go.

A pastoral peace lingered in Ferncliff Cemetery, in Hartsdale, New York, where Dominique Delong joined the greats: Judy Garland, Christopher Reeve, Jerome Kern, Joan Crawford, Jim Henson, and so many more.

I stopped talking when I heard a man talking. He looked up, caught my eye, and looked away. The Wings driver?

"Eve," I called walking up to her. "Eve," I said, hook-ing my arm through hers. "Kyle, can I borrow her for a minute?"

In the middle of conversing with people Eve and I didn't know, Kyle nodded, so I dragged Eve aside. "See that guy over there? The one with the olive suit? I think that's the Wings driver."

"You're kidding me? You can tell from his eyes?"

I chuckled. "He was like all eyes that morning, remember, and he looked guilty just now when our gazes met. But it's his voice that I remember."

"Uh, I can't tell from his eyes. Let me see if I can get behind him. I'd know that squeezable tush and those quarterback shoulders anywhere."

I rolled my eyes and smiled inwardly as she crept from tree to tree, waving as she peeked from behind each one before moving to the next. Anybody else watching her would think she needed to be committed, the ham.

Finally, she ended up in a clump of holly directly behind the guy. When she took a good assessing look at his tush, his shoulders, back to his tush, she gave me a thumbs-up.

Then she straightened her back and marched right up to him.

"Baste it, Eve. You're not supposed to give us away," I said out loud.

"Madeira, are you talking to yourself?" Phoebe Muir asked as she stopped beside me.

"Who's that guy Eve's flirting with?"

"Looks more like she's giving him hell."

"Shows how little you know Eve."

Phoebe nodded. "Okay, that's Zachary Tate. He's Lance Taggart's younger brother. Lance was Dominique's leading man in *Diamond Sands*. That's Lance in the blue suit beside Zachary. Dom considered them friends. They're not members of the Parasites, if that's what you're getting at."

I gave Phoebe a double take. "You knew about the Parasites?"

"Hey, I was Dom's girl Friday. She told me everything. Of course I knew."

I hooked my arm through Phoebe's. "Introduce me?"

Phoebe led the way and made the introductions.

"So, Mr. Deliveryman," I said to Zachary Tate. "What do you have to say for yourself?"

"I apologize for posing as a Wings delivery man?"

"And for stealing the truck?"

"I work at Wings between acting jobs," Zachary admitted. "We returned the truck."

"We?" I asked turning to Phoebe. "Aha! *You* wore the missing red wig from Dom's dressing room, didn't you, Miss Muir, in my shop that day?"

Phoebe Muir's face got pink. "Yes, yes, it was me."

"And you, Mr. Taggart, were my dreadfully overcostumed customer that morning."

"Guilty," Taggart, Dom's former leading man, said with a voice that could rival James Earl Jones. He looked older up close, not quite as perfectly dashing as his publicity photos, though his voice would carry the day in any musical.

"What was the point of that exercise?" I asked the three caballeros.

"Dom said you might be in danger after we got the gown to you," Phoebe said. "I thought we'd stick around to make sure that whoever stole the diamonds didn't follow us."

I straightened. "I'm listening."

Phoebe looked down and toyed with the tassel on her Givenchy Ombre before she looked up at me. "Something was very wrong around here, obviously, but Dominique wouldn't tell me what. She only told me to get that box to you if something happened to her. I knew she'd worked on the dress. I was afraid she was sending you the diamonds to protect them from being stolen."

I didn't tell them that those were not diamonds on the dress. I would have noticed that right away. Granted, I was shell-shocked, but I know a diamond when I see one.

"Our idea," Zachary said, "was to keep the diamonds out of the thief's hands. Well, thief or thieves."

"Do you know, or suspect, who the thief or thieves might have been?"

"No," Phoebe said, and the two brothers shook their heads. No suspects, then.

I twirled the tie at the neck of Coco's dress. "So you don't know who you were trying to protect me from?"

Phoebe shrugged and by the look of her, she felt foolish. "'Fraid not."

"I'm glad you didn't try to tackle our local detective," I said.

"We could tell you knew *him*," Taggart said. "He's here with you, right?"

"Yes, he's with my parents. I mean my father and my aunt. Hey, if you're brothers, why don't you have the same last names?"

"We're actors," Zachary said. "Stage names."

Well, that made sense, I thought. "Have you shared your suspicions about the diamond theft with the police?"

"Uh, no," Phoebe said. "There was the matter of Zack borrowing his truck without permission and driving it over a state line."

"I'm sure that Dominique is smiling down on you for a great try. I assume, since you left the Wings truck, you took the train home?"

"Not exactly," Phoebe said. "Lance and I followed the Wings truck down to Connecticut in Lance's car. After we dropped the truck off, Zack and I took the train home and—"

"I drove up north to visit a friend in New Hampshire," Taggart added.

Kyle caught up with us, shook hands with Lance and Zachary, hugged Phoebe, and put his arm possessively around Eve. "Madeira figured out your little scheme, didn't she?" Kyle said, his gaze skimming the three of them. "I told you she would."

So, Kyle knew what they were up to? Why had he said he couldn't find the gown Dom meant for me, then?

Thirty-one

Tradition doesn't make for fashion. What matters is the architecture of the garment and that architecture has to be international.

—CHANTAL ROUSSEAU

The Pierpont house was a man's manse, a tribute to the arts and crafts movement. Tiffany chandeliers like the Acorn, the Daffodil, and the Curtain Border were perfectly placed, not to mention the Grande Peony floor lamp. The priceless collection set the scene as the lamps accented authentic, antique mission-style furniture, their cushions upholstered in original earth-toned leathers.

Taupe shutters on tall, churchlike Gothic windows sat open and invited the sun to nourish the larger than life vegetation inside.

Stained-glass windows flanked the massive golden oak front door, arched at the top with straight sides, they filtered light through an entry of hanging wisteria.

Priceless art deco accents complemented the huge

rooms with coordinating oriental carpets playing off each other in greens, tans, siennas, and gingers. Art pieces of bronze and copper heralded the wealth of the Pierpont Diamond Mines.

In other words, holding the reception here had nothing to do with kindness and everything to do with showing off.

Maids and butlers circulated with trays of hot beverages and a "light" offering of shrimp cocktail, filet mignon, and lobster tails. "I sense that Pierpont would have preferred to serve champagne but doesn't dare because it'll seem more like a celebration than a wake," I whispered to Eve.

Eve looked at Kyle. "Why did Pierpont hire your mother if he didn't like her?"

"Pierpont's father, Victor, hired my mother. Victor died two weeks ago and already Pierce, the son, was closing the show."

Now I understood the closing, but I was beginning to doubt that it was losing money. It didn't matter because when the public swarms a ticket counter and buys the show out, the damn thing stays open. Pierpont would be crazy to close it now.

"After last night, he has reason to celebrate," Werner said, thinking along the same lines. "He's gonna make money hand over fist with his new leading lady."

"Speaking of whom." Eve pointed with her fork. "Is that her on Pierpont's arm?"

I raised a brow. "That didn't take long."

Werner sipped his espresso. "Unless their relationship started before Dominique was killed. Mad," Werner said, "add Pierpont to your suspect list."

"Thank you for your guidance, but I'm way ahead of you."

Pierpont and Ursula, Dom's *former* understudy approached us. "Care for a tour of the house?" the new star of *Diamond Sands* asked, acting like the hostess with no complaint from Pierpont. Do tell.

"Let's start upstairs," she said. "I love our suite."

She wanted us, Dominique's friends, to know that they, the show's backer and understudy, were sleeping together. Weird kind of misplaced pride that showed how dumb she was.

Well, maybe it was just the little girl from the wrong side of the tracks acting like she'd won the lottery.

Pierpont would have to rub that shiny new-money glow off Ursula and fast, introduce her to a little social grace, or she'd tarnish his perfect, old-money patina.

Their suite was indeed spectacular, I thought as we finished the tour. But after the second floor, I wanted more. "What's up those stairs?" I asked.

Pierce winced. "My father's rooms. They're a wreck."

"I haven't met him yet," I said, playing dumb.

Pierce looked pained but he was a bad actor. "For the simple fact that my father isn't with us any longer."

"Assisted living?" Eve asked, as if we'd rehearsed.

"No, Ms. Meyers, my father passed away."

"Quite recently," Galina Lockhart said. "Wasn't it like last month or something?"

"Two weeks ago," Ian DeLong corrected, having tagged along for the tour. "I remember because Dominique needed consoling after Victor's death."

I scoffed beneath my breath, which Ian heard and seemed to take as an insult.

Again, he was telling a half-truth, except that there was more, and less, to it. Dominique was inconsolable, I knew from being inside her skin, and Ian would not have been her choice of consolation in any case.

Kyle's expression said he agreed with my assessment, while Ian tried to take Ursula from Pierpont and failed. Weird that.

"What did your father die of?" I asked Pierpont.

"Cancer. He fought the good fight for twenty years, but it got him in the end. It came more as a relief that he was out of pain than a surprise."

Kyle's lips firmed. I'd have to ask him why later.

"Can we see the top floor?" Eve asked.

"I'm afraid not. My father's rooms are in the midst of being brought back to life."

"Too bad the same can't be said of your father," Kyle muttered, and Pierpont gave him a look so filled with venom that even Ursula stepped back.

So, I thought, there was bad blood between Victor's son and Dominique's son. Perhaps that's why they kept their feelings to themselves.

Thirty-two

Accessories are what, in my opinion, pull the whole look together and make it unique.   —YVES SAINT LAURENT

❧

We'd collected quite a group of interested celebrities during the course of the tour, so it wasn't hard for me to slip into a bathroom and pull Eve inside. I wouldn't be missed for a while.

"Now what are you up to?" Eve asked, as she checked her hair in the mirror.

I refreshed my lipstick. "I want to take a look upstairs."

Eve finger-plucked her hair spikes. "I think it's pretty clear Pierpont doesn't want us up there."

"Which is exactly why we should go, don't you think? You are my assistant sleuth, are you not?"

"Only when it's convenient. Werner and Kyle will notice that we left the group."

172

"Fine, so they can keep each other company. Shh." I held my hand in front of my lips and kept it there while the group walked back down the hall toward the stairs to the main floor. "They're gone," I whispered and cracked the bathroom door open.

Looking both ways, we sprinted across the hall and up the forbidden stairs. We *wouldn't* have wanted to go up there quite so badly, if Pierce Pierpont hadn't spent so much time explaining why we shouldn't.

All the doors off that hall were closed, so we opened them one by one. I laughed. "A bathroom with avocado fixtures. Sixties/seventies," I said. "I prefer harvest gold myself."

"My parents still have a blue bathroom upstairs," Eve said, "and a gray one down. Everything in the Meyers house was bought on sale after the color went out of style. It's my mother's way."

"I love your mother."

"So do I. Hey, this room has a bar in it with a collection of vintage bar signs, German beer steins, and a pool table. Wanna play?"

"No, we have to snoop," I said.

"Shh. Werner will hear you. Do you think this gorgeous old jukebox works?"

"If it doesn't, Tunney could fix it."

"Our meat cutter fixes jukeboxes?"

"Yep. He's a man of many talents."

Eve opened another door. "Oh," she said. "I'm going cross-eyed."

"What is it?"

"You've heard of the robe of many colors? Well, this is the den of many colors."

I caught up to her, but I stopped before I entered the room. Déjà vu all over again.

We were standing in the *Mod Squad* living room from my vision in the theater, the one in which Dominique had been wearing the gold-and-brown brocade Victorian gown and talking to Deep Throat, who I surmised to be exercising with a Hula-hoop around the corner there.

Striped walls in blues, lime, and mauve, a modern half sofa covered in huge, almost-bouncing 3D-type polka dots and rings in *nearly* the same colors.

Up close, the combination nearly made me seasick.

I rounded the infernal corner beyond which I was unable to see that day, and that's where I found the exercise equipment. Hanging on the wall, Hula-hoops, two of them. Above them hung needleworked plaques. One said "Dom's" and one said "Vic's." Seemed more like a lifetime love, someone to grow old with.

It was the comment about stealing the diamonds that didn't make sense to me anymore, especially now. Victor owned the diamond mines. Why steal them? No wonder Dominique had scoffed.

Wait, if Deep Throat was Victor, he said his cancer was gone. Had he been fooling himself? Or had someone used his cancer as a cover-up for his death?

Had Victor, like Dominique, been murdered?

Could Pierce have been responsible for Dominique's

death, because she knew so much about his father's health?

I opened the door to the adjoining room and found a bedroom as seventies as the rest of the apartment, but on the wall hung the most beautiful portrait of Dom that I had ever seen. Now that should have been at the funeral home today.

On the other hand, maybe, it should stay in the room of the man who honestly loved her. I'm not even sure why I knew he loved her, but I certainly knew how much Dom loved him. It had radiated from her as I knelt before his casket.

Dom, I thought. Are you here?

I closed the door to the bedroom, leaving it be. It seemed too sacred a place to invade.

"Eve? Did you leave?" I called. "Eve?"

"Kyle took her away," Werner said as I rounded the corner, came face-to-face with him, jumped, and screamed.

He put his hand over my mouth and shoved me in a closet.

What the—

He shook his head, his hand firm.

I held up one hand as if to tell him that I understood, and I removed his hand from my mouth myself.

He pointed to his ear. We heard people talking . . . about arresting me? The police?

"What time was it broken into?" a man asked.

Pierpont wasn't playing fair. He was trying to discredit me by making it look like I broke in.

Werner ran his hand over something near the doorjamb. Then he took out a pencil and put an X near it.

The voices receded a bit, but I heard enough to know that Pierpont was talking to his own private security guards. Because, seriously, how could he get the police to come because somebody wandered away during a house tour?

Right now, he and his security crew must be in the bedroom.

The closet in which Werner and I hid was stuffed with men's and women's designer jogging suits in assorted styles and colors. At the end of the closet, a folded sit-up board stood straight up. Werner pulled me toward it, the two of us tiptoeing through the barbells to get there.

He pushed me behind the exercise board, then squeezed his way in there with me.

Cozy. Not.

Someone opened the closet and I thought my heart would give out. Fortunately, Victor stuck to the seventies electrical code as well and no one had ever put a light switch in the closet. While one security guard shoved the jogging outfits back and forth, he dropped a barbell on his foot. He was so busy hopping and groaning that nobody looked farther than the archaic sit-up board—covered in gold plastic, behind which we hid—though it did get pushed tight against us. Werner and I were plastered together, front to front.

Eventually, Clumsy Guard closed the closet and finished his search.

"Manny," Pierpont said, "post a couple of your men in the hall, so no one can come in or out without being seen."

Wow, he had a team of security guards, but then he owned a diamond mine. No telling what treasures needed protecting.

"My father kept a fortune in antique jewels up here," Pierpont added, "and I haven't had a chance to sort them out since his death. Too painful, you understand."

"I'll post a guard," said Manny with the sore toe.

After the hall door closed, we heard their voices and footsteps receding.

My eyes had adjusted to the dark by then and I could see the guilty look on Werner's face. "Is that a Taser in your pocket," I whispered, "or are you just happy to see me?"

Thirty-three

I wanted this, I wanted to do this, but my work is me, and it has to be right.
                                                    —OSCAR DE LA RENTA

❧

Werner nearly knocked over the sit-up board trying to get out of there and away from me.

"What did you mark on the wall in there?" I asked, letting him and his physical interest off the hook. I probably shouldn't have mentioned it at all, but, well, I'm not dead or stupid.

"I found a bug," he whispered against my ear. "Somebody has this place bugged. Let's see if we can find any others, and shush while we do."

We searched, and I found one beneath the top shelf of an end table almost hidden by a leg. I raised my hand and pointed.

Werner pointed to another beneath a rowing machine.

I dragged Werner into the bedroom, and we checked

for bugs in there, but it seemed clear. The listener might be scum but at least he/she wasn't a perv.

"How are we going to get out of here with a guard posted?" I asked in a whisper.

Werner shrugged and went to look out a window. I did the same. We looked out several but the roof was full of peaks and gables, and it wasn't covered in normal shingles.

Oh no, the rich so-and-so's who built this place used what looked like blue slate or ceramic tiles, hand crafted to fit the round towers giving them the kind of texture that would catch at your clothes and break your heels.

"It does have a step-down effect," Werner said.

"I'm wearing a Coco Chanel dress, and I mean, a dress Coco herself wore."

"Your point?"

"I'd rather go out in handcuffs."

"You mean, it's valuable?"

"Museum quality." Amazingly, I caught a whiff of Dom's perfume and followed the scent. On the bedroom side of the wall, opposite the closet we'd been hiding in, the scent got strong and lingered. There I found cuts in the wallpaper, except that this cutout was in the shape of a door . . . that wouldn't budge.

I pushed a button built into only one of a set of ceramic wall sconces on either side of the door cut, and the outlined panel slid into a pocket wall. "An elevator!"

Werner whipped around.

Inside, we closed the door and pushed B, since we

assumed that meant basement, and the button sat below the other choices, like floors two and one. We'd been on three. "I'll be damned," Werner said. "Now if it doesn't deposit us into a room full of security guards, we're aced."

Werner leaned against his corner and I against mine. "Dominique's perfume is strong in here," I said. "I think she was Victor's lover. No, more than that, I think they were in love."

"And you know this because?"

"I have good instincts. I'd like to look into Victor Pierpont's death. I think Pierce lied about what killed his father. Dom led me to believe that Victor's cancer had been cured."

Well, *she had*, in a roundabout way.

The lift opened at the base of a curved, narrow, dark, metal gray staircase, in a tall, dank, light gray tower basement vestibule, plain, no frills, near what looked to be an outside door. I tried the knob. "It's locked."

"It's a deadbolt. It needs a key to unlock it from the inside." Werner nosed around the top of the door frame, the base of the stairs, ran his hands up the newel, and found that the knob finial was set inside the newel with a wide cutoff dowel. Beneath the dowel stump, he found a key and held it up for my inspection.

I silently applauded. "I'm duly impressed."

"As a cop, you see all kinds of things," he said, "like jewels in dug-up caskets," but he couldn't seem to get the key in the lock.

I took it from his nervous hand and successfully unlocked the door.

"Not a word," he said.

I saluted. Cracking the door revealed a small corner of the small backyard covered in a dusting of snow.

Werner replaced the key, followed me out, and gave me his coat. We managed to completely cross the yard along the edges of a dry-stemmed winter garden, stepping from stem clump to stem clump, so as not to leave footprints in the snow.

When two security guards came out, one of them limping—Manny—we acted like we were heading back to the house from the mermaid fountain.

"There you are," Pierpont said following them out. "When you weren't with us at the end of the tour, I wondered what happened to you. I honestly thought you'd invaded my father's private quarters, you were so curious."

"Wow," I said. "Wish I'd thought of it. I am curious. What's up there?"

"My father was a private man. He deeded me the house with a contractual stipulation that I stay out of his wing. I figured it was a small price to pay. I just went up there for the first time since his death, all contracts being void under the circumstances. Anyway, it's ugly. You didn't miss a thing. Aren't you cold?"

What a liar, I thought. He'd had the place bugged. He'd been up there all right, maybe only when his father was in the hospital, but he'd been there.

Werner put a protective arm around me. "Mad was missing Dominique and needed a minute."

"Funny," Pierpont said, "I smell Dom's perfume all over you, Madeira."

"They gave me her room last night. And I couldn't help myself this morning. Wearing a spritz of it made me feel a bit closer to her, which I needed under the circumstances."

"I didn't notice it on our tour."

"Of course you didn't. It was mixed with the perfume and aftershave everyone else was wearing."

He tilted his head in a silent "touché." "Well, come inside," Pierpont said. "We have films of Dominique that we hoped would console everyone and make them feel a bit closer to her."

He took my arm, as if he didn't trust me. I couldn't imagine why.

He sat in a chair up front to narrate and I stood in the back to mentally fit all the off-sized and oddly shaped puzzle pieces together.

"I can't believe you got out without being caught," Eve whispered, pulling me behind the stairs. "I nearly had a heart attack."

"Where were you all that time?" I asked.

"Creating a diversion to buy you some time. We got Pierpont and the security guards' attention, I'll tell you."

"How?"

"Kyle keyed Pierpont's gold stretch Lamborghini in front of the house."

Thirty-four

Red is the ultimate cure for sadness.　　　—BILL BLASS

"Don't worry about the Lamborghini," Kyle said later as we climbed the stairs to Dom's house after we dropped my father and Aunt Fiona off at the train station. "Keying the limo was my idea, and I intend to pay for having it repaired."

"I expect nothing less of you," I said, "but what excuse will you give? Like, from the kindness of your heart, you're going to—"

"Because it happened during my mother's funeral collation, which Pierpont so generously hosted, I feel it only fair that the damage expense be mine."

"Ah, okay. But I'm surprised Pierpont wasn't more furious."

"Oh, he was," Eve said. "He threatened to kill the

person who did it, which is probably why finding you in his backyard didn't faze him the way it might have earlier. He was pretty steamed when he thought you went to the top floor."

"I wonder why?" I said, cryptically. "Do you think it's possible that Pierce doesn't know about his father's elevator?" I asked Werner.

Kyle turned to us before he opened the door. "Victor had the elevator put in while Pierce was in Europe a few years ago. Victor gave Pierce's security goons a vacation and let the construction crew go to town. Father and son may have lived in the same house, but they were estranged."

"Weird arrangement if you ask me," Eve muttered.

"Victor would have given the house to charity if Pierce broke their agreement about him staying out of his father's wing."

"He did break it," Werner said. "The den is bugged, but the bedroom doesn't seem to be."

"Someday," Kyle said. "I hope that Pierce gets what's coming to him."

"Which reminds me," Werner said, turning my way. "During the movie about Dom, I found my way back to the tower, and I relocked the door from the inside."

"You ruthless housebreaker. You've arrested me and Eve for less."

"I'm a house locker, not a breaker. I should possibly be arrested for aiding and abetting, but you're the one who was snooping. I was simply trying to rescue you."

"My hero," I said, taking his arm to go inside as Nick opened the door to greet us.

"Nick, you're back. What a nice surprise. Did you find the diamonds?"

"Ladybug," he said, taking me away from Werner with an arm around my waist, "I've been looking forward to our reunion."

"After a day and a half?" I asked. "Hey, before I forget, tell the Feds that Victor Pierpont's apartment was bugged and I'm afraid he might have been murdered, too."

Nick sighed. "Shut up, Mad."

I tilted my head. "I'll bug you until you report the bugs."

"I'll do it after our reunion."

"Feeling friskier than when you left, are you?"

"Don't remind me." He lifted me in his arms and headed for the stairs.

"Hey, where are we going?" I asked, suddenly remembering Werner's clothes and luggage in my room.

"To reunite," Nick said, wiggling his brows.

"Nick, I'm pretty wrung out."

He slowed and gave me a questioning look.

I lay my head on his shoulder. "I buried my friend today."

"Ladybug, I'm sorry." His heart beneath my head slowed with his steps. In other words, he stopped thinking with his zipper brain. And after he did, he kissed my brow. "Tough day, hey? I'll take care of you."

We were not talking about the same kind of taking

care of. "How did you get back so fast? I thought you were going all the way to Plaidivostock or something?"

"Slovenia," he corrected. "I searched the plane in flight and found what Gregor and I both thought were the diamonds. But, guess what, we didn't know until we got back to FBI headquarters, here in New York, that Gregor had stuffed cubic zirconias into the ceramic vial on his person."

"Ceramic?" I asked.

"Hard to detect in an X-ray."

"Ah." Diamonds fit into small places, like pill bottles that could be stuffed into plumbing traps, ceramic vials that could be stuffed I didn't want to know where, or . . . clear glass jars, with or without gel, *like the ones somebody in a black raincoat watched Dom switch*?

If Gregor had the cubic zirconias that I originally put on the dress, what happened to the real diamonds, I wondered, and why *did* Dom switch the gel jars?

Lightbulb moment: Dominique hid the diamonds—to protect or steal them. Being Dom I suspect she wanted to protect them. Which meant that she had worn cubic zirconias for the final act the night she died. I knew because I'd seen her in her bedroom taking the CZs from their settings and replacing them with rhinestones.

Hah, I finally understood my vision from last night, the night Werner spent with me. Oh scrap, I also remembered a kiss, a zing-me-to-my-toes, curl-my-hair, fly-me-to-the-moon kiss, in my bed. I mean, Dom's bed, where I'd slept, and not alone.

Was the Wiener just generally a scrumpdillyicious kisser? Or had he known *who* he was kissing? Did that have anything to do with upping the sensuality level? Erp!

"You've gone quiet," Nick said.

I stopped biting my lip and focused on my on again's worried face. Such a gorgeous, loyal face. Guilt, guilt, guilt. "Cubic zirconias, hey?"

Dim-witted comeback, Mad, I told myself, feeling like a foolish traitor. "Call the Feds about the bugs on the third floor at Pierpont's now, will you?"

Nick set me on the floor in Dom's bedroom and made the call, and while he did, he looked around.

After he hung up, I saw the room through his eyes.

Nick went from holding his hands on his hips to sticking them in his pockets.

His actions sent a mixed message, and I found myself crossing my arms defensively.

We both looked around. Unmade bed. Men and women's clothes, including underwear, strewn everywhere. Yep, we were in a hurry all right.

It looked like hurricane Madeira had gone through here. Good one, Madeira.

Nick went to the bed to touch the indentations in both pillows. "Sleepover?" he asked.

I nodded, a little too enthusiastically, though it hadn't been *much* more than that.

"I'd buy Eve wearing men's clothes," he said, "but I don't buy her packing a *red* jock sock."

"Excuse me," Werner said, coming through the door we'd left open and snatching said jock sock from Nick's hand. "I need to pack my bags and move them upstairs."

Son of a stitch!

Thirty-five

The expression a woman wears on her face is more important than the clothes she wears on her back. —DALE CARNEGIE

❦

Nick paced at the foot of the bed, looking mighty yummy in his scruffy jeans and leather jacket, his dark hair mussed and extra wavy. "Did you two sleep together last night?" he asked.

I winced. "Define sleep."

Werner pointed to his scabbing brow. "I was unconscious. She Tasered me. I figure the floor did the rest. In my book, that's not called foreplay."

Nick's whole body relaxed. "Why did you beat the crap out of him, Mad?"

"Because I was half unconscious, myself, and there was a man coming into my room. *You* had already left."

Nick shrugged. "Why didn't you ask who it was?"

"Panic. Somebody had just called my cell phone and

threatened my life." I opened the nightstand drawer. "Then there's this."

"Give me your cell phone. We'll trace the call. I'll get the contents of that drawer to forensics, too."

I gave him my cell phone. "Thanks."

"I don't like that you were threatened."

I scoffed. "It sure weirded me out."

Werner stepped between us. "Don't you think that somebody telling Mad to go home means that she's getting close to the truth?"

"Are you saying, Detective, that you stayed with her to protect her?"

I smacked his arm with the back of a hand. "Cut the snark, Nick."

"Did you Taser him because he got in bed with you?"

"No, I Tasered him then I dragged him to the bed."

Nick eyed Werner. "You had to be dragged?"

"This is no joke, Jaconetti." I stamped my foot. "We were both nearly unconscious. First thing we knew, it was morning and Eve was barging in on us."

"Really? What did she interrupt?"

"I was concussed in my suit, thank you very much," Werner snapped.

"And you, Mad?" Nick asked. "Were you concussed in your clothes?"

"I don't like you right now, Nick, just so you know. I was wearing one of Dom's peignoir sets, at her request," I stressed, "if you must know."

Nick looked suddenly sheepish. "*Dom's* peignoir set? Okay, I get it."

"Well, I don't get it," Werner said. Not knowing about my psychometric ability to read vintage clothes, he wouldn't, of course.

Nick shut the nightstand drawer with the toe of his shoe. "I'm not usually jealous, but with us on again—"

I had to tell him about returning Werner's mighy fine kiss, even if I was half asleep. And I would someday. I crossed my arms and leaned against the window. "We're *not* on again."

Nick chuckled as if I'd made a joke. "May I see the peignoir set?"

I got the set and the note asking me to wear it, and put them in his hands, trusting he wouldn't give my psychic ability away to Werner. "We're losing track of the murder investigation," I pointed out.

Nick stared at his hand through the fabric then he looked up at me. When Nick is mad, he doesn't think, because he was brought up in a family of hotheads. Usually, he controlled himself, but his silent accusation, this was too much. "I'll thank you to take your bags and go find other accommodations."

Werner was already packing his things, but Nick's expression questioned my statement.

"Both of you," I said. "I'd like to be alone right now."

"Mad," Nick said. "I apologize. I've missed you and I—"

"Don't trust me."

"I trust you, but look at this place. We leave a room like this, after we've—"

My head came up. "Kindly refrain from finishing that statement."

Werner straightened and looked around the room.

Embarrassment warmed my cheeks. Sure, I had some questions about the kiss I remembered from my dreams, or from sleep, or whatever, but, well, Nick *should* trust me.

I held the door while the two men left with their bags. "Feel free to take the morning train tomorrow," I said. "I'll be taking a later one. I have some things to go over with Kyle before I leave."

"But shouldn't we discuss what we found in Victor's rooms, if not the entire case so far?" Werner asked. "Not that I'm an official investigator, but then neither are you, Mad."

"Thanks for pointing that out and ticking me off just a little bit more," I said. "By the time I get home, or the day after at the latest, my temper should have cooled enough for the three of us to compare notes. Get one thing clear. I wouldn't feel like talking to either of you if Dom wasn't my friend."

"Where did I go wrong?" Werner asked.

"You have a Y chromosome. Right now, that's enough. And Jaconetti, consider us very off-again."

"I guess I deserve that. Have a good trip home, ladybug."

Thirty-six

Never let your frog outdress you.   —MISS PIGGY

❧

Eve had taken the early train with the two men in my life, about whom I had mixed emotions, which, several hours later, my time on the train failed to clarify.

As we pulled into the station, I saw Werner sitting in his car waiting for me. The Wiener, my frog frickin' prince? No way.

Damn Eve for putting that shadow of doubt in my mind. I *did* remember what happened that night. Nothing. Well, a kiss . . .

I stood at the top of the train steps and glanced at the sky. Please God, Goddess—or whoever watches over concussed sleuths with itchy Taser fingers—let that night have amounted to only one hot kiss. I didn't need any more complications in my life.

Werner took my bag as I reached the edge of the platform.

"I expected Nick," I said, "but thanks for picking me up. Hey, do you have a black eye?"

He led the way to his car. "You should see the other guy."

"Not Nick?"

"No, it's from kissing the floor with my face. *You* gave me the black eye. I call it Mad Taser blue."

"Oh. Sorry."

He opened his trunk and put my bag inside, then he took a bottle of Dos Equis out of each pocket and gave one to me before he urged me to a nearby bench.

I sat in the cold winter sunshine watching people board the train, Werner beside me, my brain stuck on the fuzzy memory of a dream kiss.

Werner cleared his throat. "Nick is in DC until tomorrow, but he stopped by to apologize for his green routine before he left."

"Green as in jealous, you mean?"

"That would be correct."

Knowing Nick had been honorable made me miss him more. "He was a jerk yesterday."

Werner shrugged. "He was protecting something he holds dear."

"Aren't you the forgiving soul?" I said. "Didn't you kinda wanna hit him? I did."

Werner chuckled. "Are you going to tell him that we don't totally remember what happened the night we spent together. I mean, I had some thermonuclear dreams that night."

I came up coughing. He shouldn't have said that while I was drinking.

When Werner stopped slapping my back and I could breathe again, I was practically speechless. "I'm . . . honored?" It was the best I could manage considering my own sizzling dreams.

"Mad? Suppose you are, you know?"

"Obviously I'm not or I wouldn't be drinking this beer."

He chuckled. "Good try."

"I'm hardly the immaculate conception type and that's what it would have to have been. Let it go, Lytton."

"But suppose what I dreamed did happen and bears results."

Hot face. Hot face. "Lytton, we weren't *that* concussed."

"You mean," Werner said, speaking carefully, "you couldn't have been so concussed—read, stupid—that you might have been attracted to me?"

"I mean, so concussed that we forgot we had sex, which we didn't, because I would remember. Stop putting yourself down. You're something of a hunk, Detective, but if you tell Jaconetti I said so, I'll deny it."

Werner really looked at me then. "Tell Jaconetti? I'm taking out an ad in the program for our next class reunion."

I barked a laugh. "We slept. That's it. You know that right?"

"I can dream."

"Obviously quite well. Just as long as you know a dream is what it was."

"Didn't you dream?"

"A kiss. I dreamed a hot and excellent kiss."

"Yeah, that *was* a stunner, wasn't it?"

I elbowed him. "Stop trying to embarrass me. Your body spoke volumes when we were hiding in Pierpont's top-floor closet."

Werner ran a slow hand down his face. "Gee, thanks. I nearly managed to forget about that."

I stood and threw my empty bottle in the recycle bin while Werner downed the last of his Dos Equis and did the same.

A few minutes later, we pulled up in front of my father's house. Werner got out and came around to open my door.

"Nick and I decided that since you're determined to find Dominique's killer, and we were both with you to observe the funeral and theater at different times, we should get together to compare clues and suspects to-morrow night at his place. Are you up for that?"

"I am. What time?"

"Seven. I'll bring Dos Equis."

"I'll bring a margarita pie."

"Never heard of it."

"Think key lime pie but made with tequila and triple sec. Yum."

"Dos Equis and tequila pie sounds like the perfect way to mellow us out and even the playing field, after, you know."

"A kiss," I said. "It was only a kiss."

"Yeah, like Noah's ark was only a boat."

My father came out and welcomed me with a big bear hug. Dad's arms were where I could forget death threats and thermonuclear kisses.

"It's sure good to be home," I said. "Not that my work for Dom is finished."

My father kissed my brow. "Why isn't it?"

"I have a fashion show of her vintage clothes collection to put on for charity, and—hold on to your mortar board—I'm the executor of her will."

Werner opened his trunk as my father and I talked.

"Ms. DeLong really trusted you."

"Heck, she practically dared me to try and find her killer, like it's a game or something."

"Sleuthing again, eh?" my dad said, accepting my bags from Werner. "You approve of this, Detective?"

"I must. I chased her to New York so I wouldn't miss anything."

"Is that what you did?" I asked.

"And to see if I could find out who tried to break into Nick's house, presumably for Ms. DeLong's gown."

"Did you find anybody who might have done that?" my father asked.

Werner scratched his nose. "So many, you can't

imagine. Second to finding Ms. DeLong's killer, the attempted break-ins are another reason Nick, Mad, and I need to compare notes. See you then, kid," Werner said with a wave.

Dad and I watched him drive away.

My father carried my bags inside. "Are you hungry? Fiona came over and made dinner. She left a plate in the oven for you."

"Did she already go home?"

"Yes. She's working tomorrow. She has fewer bad nights these days, which doesn't mean she hasn't called in panic in the middle of a few."

I smiled. "Not hungry," I said. "I just want a bath and my own bed."

The minute my father set down my bags in my room and left, I called Nick.

"Ladybug," he said answering. "This is an unexpected surprise. I didn't think you were talking to me."

"I'm not. This is business." I missed him something fierce and I wished I wasn't so stubborn. Then again, he'd been a Neanderthal, and I find it hard to be treated like a possession.

I sighed. "I have psychometric readings to discuss with you before we meet with Werner tomorrow night. I'll have to be careful not to mix up fact with visions, so I need to get you up to speed with my visions."

Nick's silence spoke volumes.

"I guess we should decide how to present any nebulous but crucial clues to Werner."

"Why present them at all?" Nick asked. "He's not working the case."

"Because *somebody* sent him to New York and he got involved. Not *my* fault."

"Okay, so I may have hinted that he might find the answer to the attempted break-ins at my place if he stuck by you in New York."

"Why?"

"Because I was worried about you. With good cause, it turns out. Somebody threatened your life, ladybug." Silent pause.

"Nick? You're being eaten up with guilt, I hope."

"It's envy. That Werner was there that night and not me."

"You sent him."

"More or less. He wanted to go or he wouldn't have taken my subtle hint. Headquarters couldn't do a trace on your phone, by the way. Whoever threatened you used one of those disposable phones."

"Scrap."

"You didn't get a vision as to where the diamonds might be, did you?"

"No, but Dom did a pretty good job of playing musical gems."

"You mean, Dominique was suspicious?"

"Definitely."

"Are you home by the way? Safe?"

"Safe in my father's house."

"Good. Mad, why didn't Dominique go to the police?"

"Hell if I know."

Nick sighed. "I'll be back from DC around eleven tomorrow morning. I'll bring Chinese takeout to Vintage Magic, and maybe you can close the shop for lunch and a talk."

I didn't normally close for lunch, but I had a "be back at" clock, so I could get away with it. "Make it Thai food and you're on."

"Deal. Mad, I'm really sorry about my petty jealousy the other night."

I didn't know what to say. My personal guilt—over the kiss, and nothing more, had put as much of a kink in our relationship as Nick's suspicions, and frankly, I didn't know what to do about it. "Yeah, me, too, Jaconetti."

Thirty-seven

Be daring, be different, be impractical, be anything that will assert integrity of purpose and imaginative vision against the play-it-safers, the creatures of the commonplace, the slaves of the ordinary.
—CECIL BEATON

❧

Over our unopened Thai *and* Chinese food, Nick looked at me across the table as if I should *be* lunch.

For my part, I tried to keep my yearning to myself. I had a right to be angry. But at whom? Myself or him? Perhaps both.

Meanwhile, we had to stop drooling, start eating, and start talking about our reason for being here: my most recent visions and how they might relate to Dominique DeLong's death.

I opened the boxes and served myself. "Okay," I said to reestablish our purpose as I got up to pace, mostly so I could sit another chair length away, where his pheromones couldn't get me. "We agree that Dom was acting suspicious."

"Well," Nick said. "Suspicious of everyone around her."

"Check. And the substance that killed her might have been in her makeup, specifically in one of those small glass jars of something that might be clear skin tightening or hair gel, that she switched in one of my visions."

"The one in which you wore the trench coat."

"The black Armani trench. Yes."

"A man or a woman's coat?"

"A man's, but I found it in Dom's dressing room, so door-peeker guy must have left it there by accident."

"He might still not know where it is. Where is it?"

"I left it in Dom's vintage clothes collection closet off her bedroom."

Nick picked up his cell phone. "Brad," he said, "I got a lead on an Armani trench coat in Dominique DeLong's house, stored with her vintage clothes. Want to pick it up there and get some forensics done on it?"

Nick listened for a minute, his face pensive. "Anonymous tip. Sorry." He listened again. "Okay, good."

Nick clapped his phone shut. "A friend on the NYPD is sending a man for it right now."

I called Kyle to let him know the police were coming for the trench coat.

"Good, we can tell Werner that I saw the man's coat at Dom's, and by the size of it, I knew it didn't belong to her publicized lover, Gregor Zukovski."

Nick filled himself a plate and came to sit beside me on the fainting couch.

"You should have asked Brad if they had any leads or prime suspects, or even if they've made an arrest."

"Their prime suspects are obvious and weak: the chef, the understudy, and the ex-husband."

"I suspected them, too," I admitted. "But Werner agrees with you. They're weak. That's why I like having him to bounce ideas off of."

Nick wiped a bit of sauce off my chin and licked it off his finger.

Oy, I needed to get away from this man.

"Don't eat so fast," Nick said. "You'll get indigestion."

I'd always been a nervous eater.

"Try this." He fed me a forkful of lemon chicken.

It was like Chinese foreplay.

"So," he said, "Dominique suspected the diamonds would be stolen because she'd been approached by Deep Throat to steal them, which is probably why you saw her using decoy gems in another vision. Is that right?"

"Right. And you're going to call the New York police and the FBI to see what they know before we get together with Werner, tonight, right?"

"I hate it when you're all business, ladybug."

I stood. "You'd better be civil tonight, though Werner told me that you apologized."

"You just got home last night. How did you know?"

"You're giving me the third degree, again."

Nick put down his plate. "I don't know what's wrong with me. I'm not the jealous type."

"It's like the frickin' pheromone wars," I said not quite beneath my breath. "And I'm caught in the crossfire."

"What?" Nick looked up, his hand combed halfway through his hair, his mind miles away.

"Nothing." I had just figured out that Werner had a dangerous set of those sexy little pheromone suckers himself.

Thirty-eight

I can't afford a whole new set of enemies. —CECIL BEATON

❧

"When Werner picked me up at the train station last night, he told me that you apologized," I said. "I'm glad. No need to pout."

"I am *not* pouting."

I laughed. "You're hard to frazzle," I paraphrased from the Grinch, "but I did my best, and that's your problem."

Nick's eyes twinkled. "It's because I'm green, isn't it?"

And with that perfectly executed Grinch quote, the angst between us eased.

"I'm glad your safe room stayed safe. Maybe Phoebe and the guys were right. Somebody thinks the diamonds are in the dress box or on the dress. Somebody besides

Phoebe, Lance, or Zachary. They were in Mystick Falls the day the dress arrived at my store, but somebody else must have followed me and saw that I left the box at your house." I shivered.

"Who are Phoebe, Lance, and Zachary?"

"Phoebe was Dom's girl Friday. Zach is Kyle's friend. Lance is Zach's brother and was Dom's leading man. They got Dom's dress to me that morning. At the cemetery, after Dom's service, I figured out that they were my delivery man and customers in disguise."

"Any of their voices fit the phone threat?"

"No, the caller used a voice modulator."

"I'm sorry, but you did need a bodyguard in New York. Sending Werner was a good idea."

"Don't go there. He told me why you sent him."

"To keep you out of harm's way, as well as out of trouble, I swear."

"Don't perjure yourself." I took another helping of pad Thai noodles, pure comfort food. "My dad told me that somebody actually succeeded in breaking into your house but that the gown I made for Dominique is still in your safe room, but what about your things? Did anything of yours get stolen?"

"Between the police watching the place and the silent alarm, the guy barely got in before he was getting out. My neighbors saw an older guy in the area, red plaid flannel shirt, navy thermal vest, salt-and-pepper hair."

"I'm so sorry that storing my dress at your place got you into trouble. It's time to stand on my own. I'll have a cold storage room put in upstairs as soon as possible, with an alarm of its own."

"Mad, I like you keeping your stuff at my place."

When had he gotten this close?

"Not a good idea," I said, "especially since we're off again." I put my empty plate down and went to look beneath my counter for my chocolate stash. The bowl was empty.

Problem was, with me behind my counter, Nick had followed and boxed me in. And he kept coming closer.

Where was a cold shower when you needed one?

My doorbell rang.

"Oops. Lunch hour's over. Customers!" I pushed my way around him and unlocked the door to Dolly and Ethel Sweet. This required hugs all around. I'd never been so happy to see them.

Nick said hello to them and good-bye to me.

"We didn't mean to interrupt anything, cupcake," Dolly said with a giggle and a wink.

Ethel, the younger Sweet, at eighty, started cleaning up the remains of lunch. Dolly, her centenarian mother-in-law, looked around, gave a cheeky grin, and followed Dante, the ghost, a man that only she and I could see, down the rows of nooks until she disappeared behind him in Vive La Paris, the fashion nook farthest from us.

Later, after Ethel had refolded my shelf stock, and Dolly returned giddy and pink-cheeked from her assignation with the ghost she'd had an affair with last century, I asked her to make a margarita pie for me to bring to Nick's that night.

"I don't know, cupcake," Dolly said, "that pie's a lot of work."

"Mama, it is not," Ethel said, scandalized. Dolly made a habit of scandalizing her daughter-in-law. It was one of her favorite sports.

"I'll pay you," I said.

"What do I care? I'm rich and too old to spend what I've got."

"Watch it," Dante warned me, chuckling. "She wants something."

Didn't I know it. "If not money, what do you want to trade for the pie?"

"I want to model one of Dominique DeLong's vintage dresses during the fashion show you're giving for her charities. And if George Clooney is there, I want an introduction . . . and a kiss."

"Whoa," Dante said.

"Hey," the plucky centenarian said. "*I'm* still *alive*."

Dante winked. "You certainly are."

Thirty-nine

Fashion design is a functional art. It's an art you can actually touch and feel and interact with and not be afraid to wear.
—REBECCA TURBOW

❧

That night, Werner showed up at Nick's with three six-packs of Dos Equis, and I was happy to tempt the two pheromone spritzers with margarita pie.

Things were strained, at first, because of that show-down in Dom's bedroom, Nick versus Werner, but the beer, and the extra dose of tequila in the pie, chilled us out by the time we took out our notes.

The two men agreed that I should go first, and since they agreed, I did, too.

"I'm not going to bore you by repeating what we all saw together," I said, "but I will share a few of my personal observations and deductions, if you don't mind."

Nick tilted his head and Werner remained poker-faced.

"First of all, Kyle told me a little while ago that Zander Pollock, Dominique's personal chef, showed up to pack his bags and move out of his apartment there. He'd been a prime suspect but when the medical examiner's official report came in, it proved that no peanuts were found in Dom's stomach, so we can cross Pollock off our lists.

"He was never on mine," Werner said.

Nick shrugged. "Mine, either."

"So glad you two agree on something. But it seems to me that if a cook wanted to kill someone, he wouldn't do it with food he cooked himself. He could have killed her some other way."

Nick raised his bottle of beer. "Mad one, Nick and Werner zero!"

Werner tapped Nick's bottle with his and they both drank to me.

"Are you mocking me?" I asked.

"Great beer," Nick said.

Okay, so they agreed on two things. But were they ganging up on me and when had I gone paranoid? When I kissed one and was procrastinating about telling the other?

I shook away the ridiculous thought. "Nick, since the medical report has come in, what did you find out when you called the police and FBI this afternoon?"

Did Nick cringe? "They're doing a sound analysis on your threatening phone call. I hope you got another phone."

"I've got Dad's for now, thanks. Anything else? Any new suspects?"

"Our suspects pretty much clammed up on the phone," Nick said. "I'm more charming in person."

Werner's bottle hit the table. "Not always."

"Stop it," I said, cutting them off at the pass. "Did either of you notice Ian DeLong's crooked baby finger?"

Werner chuckled and Nick shook his head.

"Okay. I get it. You don't look at other men. Well, I do, and here's the scoop. Ursula Uxbridge has the same crooked baby finger, same hand, same shape as Ian DeLong. Galina Lockhart is her mother. My guess is that Ian cheated on Dominique with Galina and that Ursula Uxbridge, Dom's understudy, is their love child."

"Your point?" Nick asked. "This isn't a soap opera."

"Her point," Werner said, "is motive. Galina's motive would be jealousy. She's known for despising Dominique. Getting Dom out of the way would be a powerful motive for her own acting career, not to mention getting her daughter the starring role in *Diamond Sands* as an added bonus."

I nodded. "Right in one, Detective."

Nick crossed his arms, and the look he gave me shivered me to my toes, warm bedroom eyes full of promise. "Jealousy is powerful," he said. "Makes people do stupid things."

"Apology accepted." I nodded and flipped the page on my notebook. "What about Gregor? Was he working on his own do you think? Or was he getting what he thought were the diamonds out of the country for himself *and* a few partners?"

Werner ruminated on that.

Nick sat across from me. "We gave Zukovski a chance to give us his partners' names for a "get out of jail free" card, and he didn't take it. I think he was working alone. He saw his chance when Dominique collapsed and grabbed the diamonds, which she always wore glued to her face like a mask in the last act, before the ambulance left the theater.

"The real killers, I suspect, pulled over on their way to the hospital planning to take the diamonds from her in the stolen ambulance only to find that the diamonds were already gone."

"Who called nine-one-one?" I asked.

Nick shrugged. "Nobody seems to know."

"Or they're not talking. Can you run voice recognition software on that call?"

"Done. Same setup as your call."

Nick opened another beer. "Zukovski's plan sucked. That's why I caught him so fast. The real killers were more thorough in their planning—not counting Zukovski's last-minute theft—which is why we haven't nailed them yet."

"You caught Zukovski because he's dumb?" Werner said. "Doesn't say much for your skills."

I was afraid they were going to get into it again. "What about Ursula Uxbridge, herself?" Nick asked, ignoring Werner's taunt. "Same motive: the lead role in an off-Broadway production?"

I shook my head. "I don't think she can spell motive, much less plan a murder. However cozy she looked on Pierce Pierpont's arm, that was an act. Pierce was using Ursula to tick off Ian—her father—and Ursula lapped up the diamond magnate's attention. She's a bit of a pin tuck. No substance and more than a few stitches short of a seam. Murder seems too complicated for her, career or not."

"Madeira Cutler," Werner said, shaking his head. "I do believe that you're a natural-born sleuth, whether I think you should be or not."

Forty

Whether it's the past or the present, all my ideas come from
what's going on around me . . .   —ANNA SUI

"Thank you, Werner. I'll take that as a compliment. A
natural-born sleuth, hey? Hear that, Jaconetti?"

"I do, and I'd like to throw natural-born vixen into the
pot. You're enjoying us butting heads over you, aren't
you?"

What girl wouldn't? "Are you butting heads over *me*?
I hadn't noticed."

Both men cracked a smile.

"I mean, why would you?" she asked on second
thought. "It's friendly head butting, isn't it? Which is
definitely better than the other kind."

"If you're fishing for compliments," Nick said, "you
won't get them here. You're one scary sleuth."

I raised my chin. "A sleuth *should* scare the perps."

Werner chuckled. "But should she scare the police and the FBI?"

Nick gave Werner a nod. "Good point. She's pretty much a loose cannon when it comes to sleuthing, don't you think?"

"Hey, are you calling me a flake behind my back, right in front of me?"

Nick tried to look innocent. "Only on some points."

"But you're smart and amusing, too," Werner said.

"And we both want what's best for you, ladybug, so think of us as covering your back."

"Damned straight," Werner added. "And the head butting, that's us jostling for position back there."

I stood to look down at them, my hands on my waist. "Damned if your abuse didn't end up sounding like a compliment. Anyway, murder case, remember? Try this clue on for size. I think Gregor Zukovski was a decoy."

Werner stood and stretched his legs. "A decoy. Good point. He could have taken those diamonds where?"

"Plaidivostock," I said.

Nick growled. "Slovenia!"

"Okay, don't get your boxers in a bunch."

Werner coughed. "He could have taken the *fake* diamonds to Slovenia to throw the police off the trail while the real diamonds were being stashed somewhere else."

"Lytton, you're good. I never thought of that."

Werner looked surprised. "Isn't that what you meant by decoy?"

"No, I meant that Gregor was a decoy boy toy. Dominique didn't love him. She was in love with Victor Pierpont."

"Ah," Werner said. "The old double-decoy routine."

Nick gave Werner the old double take. "Victor Pierpont? Do you mean *Pierce* Pierpont?"

"No, Pierce is Victor's son. Dom loved Pierce's father, Victor, who died two weeks ago. He lived upstairs at the Pierpont Mansion in a retro seventies apartment."

"Why didn't I know about this?" Nick asked.

"Because you went to Plaidivostock and missed the funeral. Pierce told me, personally," I added, "that his father died of cancer, but that was a bald-faced lie. Dom told me that Victor was cancer free after his treatment. Nick, can you have the FBI take a look-see into *Victor's* death?"

Nick sat straighter. "On what evidence or at least on what veneer of pretense? They need a reason to investigate. Tax dollars and all that."

"What, the death of a millionaire diamond mine owner who supposedly died of cancer when he was cancer free isn't enough? You've got motive: His son lied about what killed him. So they match his medical records to cause of death. Can't cost the taxpayers that much."

Nick flipped open his cell and made a few calls. "What else do you have?" he said when he was done, looking from me to Werner.

"Don't look at me for answers," Werner said. "I was only there to keep Mad out of trouble."

"Fat lot of good you did," Nick mumbled. "You got her into trouble."

"Hell-lo. I'm in the room. And that's another bone I have to pick with you, Jaconetti. What's with sending a babysitter to look after me? *Whatever* happened between me and Werner is your own fault, you know."

"Excuse me," Nick said. "Did you say: *whatever*? Do you mean to tell me that you don't know? Either of you?"

Werner and I exchanged glances. We knew what we knew, and I needed to fess up about that kiss.

"I didn't mean to tell you anything," I snapped. "Now stop trying to change the subject. You didn't trust me and that could put me off you like . . . for a very long time."

Or ten minutes if we were alone together.

Forty-one

I liked the whole feeling . . . that everything was about to happen, that there were so many possibilities. —ANNA SUI

❧

The day for Dominique's charity vintage fashion show finally arrived with too many suspects and no clear murderer in sight.

Everyone buzzed at the Vancortland House, a Mystic riverfront mansion with a glossy marble façade and Gothic arched windows. How easy was it for me to get the place for the event? Easy-peasy lemon squeezy. My sister's father-in-law, Justin Vancortland IV, owned it.

Today, its second-level diamond-pane windows winked like conspirators in the winter sun glinting off the water.

At least that was the sight that greeted me after the twenty-four-karat gates opened, parting a central pair of kissing swans and breaking the heart made by their necks.

To give them their due, those swans allowed us into a world that just might be a worthy backdrop to showcase Dominique DeLong's famous and outstanding designer vintage clothing collection.

Yes, today I was hosting Dom's posthumous fashion show, highly publicized, of course, and every fashionista in the free world would be crossing the drive beside a snow-dusty garden, spiraled shrubs, sleepy weeping cherry trees, and an angel fountain whose rainbow mist had taken the winter off.

In the grand foyer—remarkable for its French crystal chandelier and its floor worked in a royal-blue-and-gold fleur-de-lis mosaic—I had two hundred matching chairs placed in a three-quarter circle facing an ultrawide curved staircase straight from *Gone with the Wind*.

Tonight, each model wearing one of Dom's vintage outfits would descend the stairs and pose for the guests while outside spotlights sent artificial gaiety cascading through the colorful Tiffany glass in the floral-scape windows on the first floor.

Because Dominique planned this to pull money in for her two favorite children's charities, she had recorded a medley of vocals specifically for the occasion, and the CD would be given to each of the guests before they left.

I read the list of songs on the back of the crystal case: "Monday's Child," "Pass It On," "This World Is What We Make It," "Mighty Like a Rose," "Little by Little," "Children Need a Helping Hand," and "Carry On."

Well, I thought, if Dom's songs don't wring a few donations out of these wealthy vintage clothing aficionados, nothing will.

At five hundred dollars a ticket, you'd think the pickings would be slim, but fortunately, I rented fifty extra chairs for the overflow. Then we had to bring in chairs from all over the house. "Gee, Cort, I never thought I'd say this, but your foyer is too small."

My sister Sherry, radiant in her pregnancy, hugged her husband Justin's arm and laughed. "See, and you always thought it was too big."

My brother-in-law rolled his eyes.

"Don't tell your sister Brandy it's too small," Cort said. "I promised her she could use the place for a fundraiser when she comes home next month." He lifted his granddaughter, Vanessa, into his arms because she was asking Sherry to pick her up, and she was just too heavy for that to be safe at this stage of Sherry's pregnancy.

Cort had also promised me that I could use the place for Sherry's shower, which is another reason Brandy was coming home next month, but we didn't want Sherry to know that.

Vanessa, three years old, and excitement personified, was wearing her best red plaid party dress with matching shoes and purse, another impetuous fashionista in the making.

"Well, Brandy can use the ballroom," I said. "For my part, I chose your spectacular staircase in lieu of a runway."

"Am I wrong?" Cort asked, "or are there a few big-name celebrities in my house?"

"I'll say." Sherry put a hand to her back, which was my brother-in-law Justin's cue to get her to her seat.

I kissed her cheek before Justin led her away. "You have lots of celebrities in your house, Cort, and here come two more," I said. "Cort, this is Melody Seabright from *The Kitchen Witch* show. She's the founder of the Keep Me Foundation. And this is Kira Fitzgerald Goddard representing St. Anthony's Home for Boys."

"It should be for girls, too," Vanessa said.

"We're building one for the girls," Kira said. "The Bessie Pickering Hazard Home for Girls. My husband's grandmother started the foundation to support St. Anthony's, so we're naming our sister school after her."

Vanessa beamed. "That's okay then."

Vancortland, Cort for short, shook their hands. "Welcome to my home. Vanessa, will you show our guests to their seats in the front row?"

Fiona was already upstairs among the models when Eve came in. "You look gorgeous in that feminine steampunk look," I said. "Seriously. The style *is* you. I was wrong when I said it wasn't."

"If you make me blush, I'll personally throw you into the Mystic River, and this time, I won't jump in after you."

"Right. Sorry. No compliments. Did you remember to bring me a robe for between changes? I'm so mad I forgot mine and so glad that I caught you before you left home to bring one for me."

"Yep, it's the black one I bought at your shop the other day while you were bringing Dom's dress to Nick's," Eve said. "Well, I'd better scoot up the elevator to join the other models. I'll throw the robe over a chair in plain sight." Eve took the stairs as Werner came our way.

"Is Nick coming?" he asked.

I chuckled. Nick's exact words when I asked him were: "Not if you Tasered me."

Werner took my arm and propelled me into the nearest den, looked around, and invaded my personal space.

"Have you told him about the kiss?" His jaw got tense.

"Oh, for pity's sake, it was only a kiss. A chaste kiss."

"A kiss, yes. Chaste? Not hardly."

"So you agree it was nothing more?"

"Just tell me when I can stop worrying Nick'll take a swing at me."

"Yesterday. Last week. Next Tuesday. Never. Fagedaboutit!"

Men!

Forty-two

It is all magical. I always look at nature and I think nature has the most beautiful colors. I always like to have colors in my designs, like the flowers and the sea, that make life.

—VIVIENNE TAM

The Parasites had come to the fashion show, I realized as I stood up to begin. Even Chef Zander Pollock came, "for Dominique's sake," he said. He had prepared the canapés for before the show and the dessert, to be served afterward.

Once Nick's background check on Pollock revealed nothing incriminating or suspect, I accepted his offer.

"Before we officially begin the Dominique DeLong Memorial Vintage Fashion Show, I'd like to introduce Melody Seabright, founder of the Keep Me Foundation, which helps young, unwed mothers to keep their babies, and Kira Goddard, a member of the family who founded St. Anthony's Home for Boys who need parents."

Vanessa, to the side, put her arm around Cort's leg

and leaned into him. With her mother, Cort's daughter, being hospitalized indefinitely, Cort had become Vanessa's family. I imagine that she felt the sting of being without a mother, more or less.

Cort picked up his little one and cuddled her until her smile grew and her cares vanished.

Melody and Kira took center, er, foyer, and gave the attendees a brief overview of their respective charities, both mentioning how much Dominique had meant to them, and how deeply she would be missed.

They presented a short slide show in which Dominique interacted with the boys at St. Anthony's and with the Keep Me Foundation's teen mothers and their new babies.

The soundtrack for the slideshow was a recording of Dominique singing "Children Need a Helping Hand."

I gotta tell you, seeing my friend loving those kids, hearing her gentle, caring voice sure gave me a lump in my throat.

After the presentation, Dom's music continued while I gave Kyle a set of index cards. "I numbered them," I told him, "in case you fumble or drop them."

"I should be insulted, but I'm that nervous. I'd be less intimidated by a room full of stockholders out for blood, or even an angry board of directors."

I squeezed his arm. "As each girl comes down the stairs, read the name of the item at the top of the card. They'll do three poses here in the circle at the base of the stairs. Read the descriptions in order, one description for each pose."

"Got it," he said. "And what will you be doing?"

"Coordinating the models as they change their outfits."

"Can we switch jobs?" he asked as I walked away and grabbed little Vanessa by the hand.

I smiled as the elevator took us upstairs to the chaos I knew was waiting for me.

My models belonged to me and to Dominique: Phoebe Muir, Dom's girl Friday; Rainbow Joy, her hairdresser/ makeup artist; Galina Lockhart, a rival ingénue and actress, and mother of Dom's understudy; Ursula, the understudy herself; Quinny Veneble, Dom's catty best friend, mother of Phoebe; Dolly Sweet, centenarian; Eve, my BFF; Aunt Fiona, my mother's BFF; oh, and me.

I was the only one not dressed in my first outfit. Theirs I had marked with their names and #1 on the temporary paper shrouds I'd slipped over each outfit. "Okay, Vanessa," I told Cort's granddaughter. "Go down and tell Kyle we're ready to begin."

This, I knew, would be my last moment of sanity. Changing into the second go-round of outfits on the run would cause chaos to the max.

"Phoebe? Need any adjustments? You're first."

"Nope. I'm all set."

"Okay, then, the music has been turned down, so it makes a fine background for the show and people will be able to hear the outfits' descriptions. Go."

Galina came to me looking for a repair on an Elsa Schiaparelli linen jacket with an embroidered motif of a woman with gold sequined curls flowing down her right arm, done after a motif by Jean Cocteau, circa 1937. "Just half a snap missing," I said. "Hold it closed."

When she did, I saw her hand. "That's a gorgeous ring," I said.

Galina preened. "It's a diamond and gold cigar band initial ring. Someone I care about very much gave it to me."

I tried to sew quickly, but my stomach flipped, and I had trouble keeping my balance. Suddenly, I was Dominique wearing the Schiaparelli jacket, and I heard several people, on the opposite side of a dressing room door, talking in hushed tones about "the diamonds," speaking at the same time, but somehow between them, repeating, almost word for word, the proposition Victor had made about stealing them. Oy, I was, of course in Dominique's space, again.

I, I mean Dom, began to panic. How could they do that? Would I be wearing the diamonds when they tried to steal them? The show diamonds were either locked up or in my possession. There was no in between.

Only one thing to do, I—no, Dominique thought. Hide the diamonds.

"She's okay," Eve said, helping me up. "Have you been too busy to eat again today, Mad?"

"'Fraid so, Eve. Galina?" I asked. "Does the jacket snap now?"

"Yes." Galina looked satisfied. "I guess it's nearly my turn."

I watched Galina take the stairs as Eve shoved a cup of juice to my lips. "What did you see?" she whispered furiously.

I took the cup from her hand and drank the juice. "What did I see?" I asked myself. "The beginning of the end, I think."

"Scary," Eve said.

"You have no idea."

Forty-three

The dress must not hang on the body but follow its lines.
When a woman smiles the dress must smile with her.
—MADELEINE VIONNET

I took my seafoam gown out by the hanger and hoped beyond hope that I wouldn't get a vision and see Dom's painful and gruesome death or something, though how could that be if she died during the final act and my dress had not been a costume in the show?

I might be safe.

Figuring that out made me feel a little less shaky and a lot more confident. Maybe I *wouldn't* zone and fall down the stairs. Not that I'd ever played it safe.

My mother told me as much after I jumped off the *Charles W. Morgan*, Mystic Seaport's famous whaling ship, when I was in kindergarten, to retrieve the purse that matched my jumper.

I proved it when I called Werner a Wiener in third

grade, then I really proved it in high school when I snuck Nick Jaconetti up the getaway tree outside Brandy's bedroom, so he could spend the night and leave via the tree before dawn.

Damn, I missed Nick.

I slipped over my head the sleeveless silk seafoam gown I'd designed and made so long ago when I was a fan hyperventilating over the adored Dominique De-Long, making sure not to catch my hair, or a fingernail, in any of the rows of gems aligned with the neck and sleeves.

As I expected, since the dress was cut on the bias, it made love to my curves and adapted itself to mine in the same way it had adapted itself to Dom's.

I had never expected to wear this dress, but Dom asked in her instructions that I model it. Yes, I was chancing a vision, but I was doing this for her.

When Quinny exited the elevator wearing a black Claire McCardell "baby doll" dress, circa 1946, I knew it was my turn.

As I walked down the Vancortland stairs while Kyle described the dress, naming me as the designer and creator, exclusively for Dominique DeLong, I got a pretty good collective "ah" from the audience, people who knew me, I expected.

But then I got a flashback to Dom's gut-wrenching fear as she replaced the cubic zirconias with rhinestones. I gasped, grabbed the stair rail with one hand, and slapped my other hand to my heart.

That's when it happened.

Half the rhinestones fell like a waterfall down the stairs, tinkling all the way.

My first thought: Great, they'll think I'm a slipshod dressmaker.

My second thought: Why were Ian DeLong and Lance Taggart on the stairs scrambling over each other to collect the rhinestones?

Another flashback and an answer from Dom: "Because they think they're the missing diamonds and they don't want to lose a one."

There was more than my psychometric ability at work here. Dom was trying to help me find her killer. I'd never missed her more.

As for the gems, I knew diamonds, but I hadn't looked that closely at any point in time, not after I got the news that Dom died, certainly, and not after I saw Dom put the rhinestones in. But suppose I *missed* a gem switch along the way?

Had I just let loose a rain of diamonds?

For me, the fashion show was ruined. "Gentlemen," I said to the greedy miscreants, or murderers, at my feet, "you're hampering the proceedings. This is a fashion show. Last I knew, being adored isn't part of the script."

The women in the audience chuckled.

These men thought they knew something I didn't. I knew now that Dom led her murderers on a merry chase, and she wasn't finished with them yet, not even from the grave.

I picked up a gem myself. Yep, a wild-goose chase, more fool them. This was not a diamond.

"I apologize, ladies and gentlemen, for the interruption. I shouldn't have included the dress in the show, once I knew that Dominique, an outstanding Broadway actress but a shoddy seamstress, replaced the stones herself. Thank you for your patience."

I motioned Werner over and led him from the room so the fashion show could continue. "Detective, would you please relieve the gentlemen of their diamonds."

Yes, I'd described them as diamonds on purpose. It was called bait.

I counted the empty settings on my dress. "Werner, between them, they should have fifty."

I watched until Werner did a count and gave me a nod.

I opened my hand for the diamonds, closed my fingers over them, and watched Lance and Ian stare at my hand as I did.

"Mad," Werner said, "I'd like to detain these characters, if you don't mind, just long enough to have the guys at the station run a check on them."

"Be my guest," I said, unable to hide my smile.

I made a spectacle of myself getting into the elevator in front of everyone, and halfway up, in the dark behind an ornately gilded elevator gate, I heard the crowd burst into applause.

I sighed. Not such a catastrophe after all. That made me feel a bit better. Knowing that Ian and Lance thought

I had the diamonds, however, scared the hell out of me. Because they were likely Dom's murderers and they knew that I saw through their thoughtless greed.

I misled them on purpose saying the rhinestones were diamonds. I hope the gamble I just took with my life was worth the risk. I prayed that because of it, I found Dom's killers, plural, because I was beginning to think there had to be more than one.

Cort came up and gave me a leather case for the rhinestones and let me lock them up in a bedroom safe, bless him. But I couldn't tell even him the truth. Not yet.

I didn't have to walk the stairs/runway for another half hour, in Coco Chanel's very own little black dress, to end the show. So for now, I could breath easy.

Dolly modeled a fitted, long-sleeved gray pinstripe Givenchy wool dress with a full front placket and four self-bows. "Dolly, that makes you look seventy-five again."

"Can you find an outfit that will take another thirty years off? I'd wear it to your shop."

Her giggle entertained Cort and he laughed, too.

"Go and strut your stuff, you cheeky babe," I said.

She positively glowed as she went down the stairs on Cort's arm, and she did it with style.

When I heard the guests applaud, I peeked around the corner and saw that she'd gotten a standing ovation. Even Cort stepped aside to applaud her.

I was still smiling when I took off the seafoam gown and hung it up. Then I grabbed the black robe over one of the stuffed chairs, slipped it on, sat in the chair, lay my head back, and closed my eyes for a rejuvenating minute.

In less than a second, I knew that rejuvenation was not to be.

I stood looking down at the top of a round oak table. Near a quarter-moon-shaped scratch, I saw a large jar, not of a skin-tightening gel. This jar had a name: Samson's Body Glue. The labeled container sat surrounded by half a dozen small empty jars *exactly* like the jars Dom switched in her dressing room.

Clear gel. Body glue. Diamond glue.

Beside the large jar sat a diamond-shaped early American pressed-glass salt cellar with a tiny green glass ladle to match.

Inside the salt cellar: four peanuts.

Forty-four

Clothes can suggest, persuade, connote, insinuate, or indeed lie, and apply subtle pressure while their wearer is speaking frankly and straightforwardly of other matters.

—ANNE HOLLANDER

I had zoned, but I didn't know why, didn't know who I was. I saw my hands, small, bony, with scratched pink polished fingernails chewed to the quick. My knuckles went white as I grasped the edge of the oak table because my neck hurt so badly.

Someone was pushing my head forward with a vengeful grasp on my neck, so I couldn't look anywhere but down, at the table, at the jars, and ladle, at the sleeve of my black robe.

"This is no time to change your mind," someone whispered furiously. "You're not alone in this. Just do it."

I did it. I picked up the tiny green glass ladle, scooped up a peanut from the salt cellar and dropped it in the large jar of body glue . . . the glue that would adhere Pierpont's diamonds to Dominique's face tomorrow night for the last time.

When I finished and put the tiny ladle down, I thought I might throw up.

I saw a man's hand pick up the ladle, and on his costume uniform cuff, a Royal Air Force button. That hand didn't hesitate to drop a peanut into the body glue. "Take that, bitch," he said with a voice that could rival James Earl Jones.

Another peanut got dropped in with a flourish. "She wouldn't be a DeLong if it wasn't for me!"

The last got fumbled and dropped and had to be caught by a shaking hand with a diamond and gold cigar band ring, G. L. L. engraved in the center.

During that fumble, I got a peek at the aging linoleum floor in the dressing rooms at the theater.

I opened my eyes and saw that several of the models were watching me. "Did you have a good sleep?" Phoebe asked. "We hated to wake you but the show's almost finished, and you have to put on the Chanel dress for the finale."

"Oh sure." I stood up and saw that there was another black robe on a different chair. "Eve, which is the robe you brought for me?"

"Sorry," Eve said, "but it's not the one you're wearing."

"That's my robe," Rainbow Joy said. "No problem. I don't mind that you wore it."

I picked up Rainbow Joy's hand and ran my finger over her purple nail polish. "Pretty color, but you should stop biting your nails."

"Dominique used to say that I'd get an infection if I didn't stop."

"Well," I said. "You showed her."

Rainbow paled and took a quick step back, before she shook her head, denying the venom in my statement.

I finished the fashion show in Coco's gown, accepted everyone's congratulations, and ate crème brûlée in a daze.

Melody and Kira had gotten a great many donations from the vintage clothing collectors and big checks from Cort. But *I* felt as if I existed in a parallel universe.

I knew Dominique's murderers and they were, all four, here at the fashion show . . . watching me. They knew where my shop was. They were going to be outside when I left tonight.

Unless I stayed here. Cort would let me. Sherry and Justin were staying.

I needed to tell someone who could do something about this, but I didn't want to ruin Dominique's show with a scandal or lower the donations for the charities, as people were still writing checks.

Werner came my way. *He* might be able to keep me safe, if I could figure a way to act like I needed protecting.

Nick knew about my psychometric ability, and sure, he thought I was nuts at first, until I proved myself. But telling Werner? No. No way. Never.

I sure wished Nick had come tonight despite the fact that he'd rather be Tasered than attend a fashion show. I mean, he could have come just to support me, though he did say he had paperwork for the Bureau to do.

I know, he'd attended some boring cocktail parties with people in the fashion industry, but, well, this was different. This was my show, for my dear friend.

"Mad," Werner whispered, "don't you think you should get that dress with the diamonds on it to the New York police?"

"Why?" I asked. "Dom gave it to me."

"They're stolen diamonds."

I couldn't screw with him anymore than I'd already been forced to do. I excused myself to the people waiting to talk to me and walked Werner a bit away from the crowd. "Can I be honest with you?"

"Of course. Anytime."

I pulled him into the family dining room, the small one, which only sat twenty people, and shut the door.

"Those aren't diamonds on the dress. They're rhinestones."

"But you called them diamonds."

"Did you see the way Lance Taggart and Ian DeLong jumped to pick them up? *They* think they're diamonds, which means they might have murdered Dom. I let them think they were right so I could watch their reactions."

"That doesn't sound very smart."

"Yeah, I've figured that out. Can you drive me home?"

"Sure. I'll even bring you back for your Element, tomorrow."

"Right, I need my car for Dom's vintage clothes. I chose the Element because it could hold so many. I'm bringing them back to New York when I drive in for the reading of the will late tomorrow afternoon."

"Bring one vintage dress with you now, will you?" Werner asked. "Bring the one with the fake diamonds. That way Cort's house won't be a target. Carry it out on a hanger so everybody can see it."

"Good idea, except that would make us targets."

"I know, Mad. I have a worse-case-scenario plan. Trust me?"

"I do." Surprisingly.

Sherry had already gone up for the night by the time I got back out there to mingle with my guests. Melody and Kira would let me know how well we did, because some people took home brochures, so it wasn't over.

Eve and Kyle left right before we did, and Eve's wink at me said she had plans. Kyle looked quite pleased to climb into my best friend's less than large but quite sporty little Mini Cooper and be taken anywhere she cared to take him.

I was happy for them.

It wasn't long into our drive down the winding ocean road that Werner took a turn I didn't expect.

"What are you doing?"

"We're being followed," he said. "By some old car."

"Two-tone silver 1953 Bentley limo?"

Werner gave me a double take. "What are you, a car savant?"

"It belongs to DeLong Limited. It's Ian DeLong."

"Or Kyle," Werner said.

"I wouldn't be *afraid*, if it was Kyle."

"Maybe you should be."

Forty-five

Souls wouldn't wear suits and ties, they'd wear blue jeans and sit cross-legged with a glass of red wine. —CARRIE LATET

❧

"Where are you taking me?" I asked Werner.

"Since we can't shake the DeLong car, I'm arresting you. Murderers rarely try to break into jail. Do you have any evidence that they're Dominique DeLong's murderers, by the way?"

Admissible evidence? "Only their greed and panicked idiotic eagerness to pick up the rhinestones. What are you charging me with?"

"Possession of stolen diamonds."

"They're not diamonds."

"Doesn't matter. Bring the dress. Eventually, a diamond expert will prove you right."

"Not anybody from Pierpont Diamonds, please. You and I sort of pissed them off after the funeral.

Ask them to get somebody from De Beers or Tiffany, please."

"Primo thought." Werner glanced my way. "With an honest diamond expert, the charges will be dismissed."

"You don't sound convinced."

"You scare me, but my uncertainty in this circumstance ranks right up there with nebulous dreams."

"Ah, so you know now that they were nebulous?"

"Maybe I just wished they were real."

"I could beat you for not letting Eve's moronic comment of that morning go."

Werner grinned. "I dare you."

"Here it comes: Wiener, Wiener, Wiener!"

He barked a laugh as he pulled into the police station parking lot, while Dom's Bentley kept going, thank God.

I couldn't help myself. I laughed with him. I guess that's what friends did.

Werner came around to let me out. I carried the seafoam diamond dress in plain sight for anyone who might have been watching: Ian DeLong for one.

"Book her, Billings. Possession of stolen diamonds."

"Oh, that's why you were laughing," Billings said as he pulled out a chair for me at his desk.

I touched Billings' arm. "Thanks for not using cuffs."

"Hey, I took you to our eighth-grade dance," Billings said. "I can catch you if you run, and I'm pretty sure you won't turn into Super Fashionista and fly away. I also know that you wouldn't steal any diamonds."

"After he books you, Mad, call your father, or who-ever, to bring you an overnight bag and a blow-up bed you'll be comfortable sleeping on. I have to work on extraditing you to New York."

"What!"

"Tomorrow morning, I drive you in a police car, two ahead of us, two behind, as escorts, in case the '53 Bentley appears on the road."

My fists found my hips. "And I get put in jail in New York City? Are you crazy?"

"Nope. I'm calling ahead. They'll have a diamond expert waiting, the charges will be dismissed, and we'll get them to bring you to the DeLong residence, where you can prep for the reading of the will. Also, we get to give them any clues we can think of. Time to pull out that little ditty about Ian DeLong being the father of the understudy."

"I already told Nick, who told the FBI, but it won't hurt to repeat," I said, "plus it might shed more suspicion on Galina Lockhart, the understudy's mother. I wouldn't be surprised if she was in on it." She so was.

Now if I could only shed some light on Lance Taggart and Rainbow Joy, I'd be in, though Rainbow wanting out at the last minute might work in our favor, I thought.

The expression on her face when I made that comment about getting Dom back sure looked like guilt to me. Sick-to-her-stomach guilt. Plus, if she admitted she was coerced into going along, the police might be willing to cut a deal. But I couldn't get *that* ball rolling. Only Rainbow Joy could do that.

And who the hell owned the black trench coat I was wearing when I saw Dom switch the small jars of body glue? He must be in on it, too, or Dom would have gotten away with it. I couldn't wait to see if the police knew who owned the coat.

I called Aunt Fiona and described the outfit I wanted to wear for the reading of the will tomorrow, then I asked for an air mattress and an overnight bag.

I could hear my father blustering and shouting in the background. "Gee, I hope I didn't interrupt anything."

"Only a DVD of *Hamlet* and a running commentary on Will Shakespeare. Did you know that he and your father were on a first name basis?"

"Give me that phone!" my father snapped. "Madeira Cutler, what have you gotten yourself arrested for this time?"

Forty-six

A man hasn't got a corner on virtue just because his shoes are
shined.

—ANN PETRY

Dad, Aunt Fiona, and Nick arrived at the police station
together, Nick feeling guilty because I didn't call him
when I was in trouble.

Werner and I told them what went down.

Nick paled and took my hand to stand me up. "I'm
sorry I let you down. I should have come, my paperwork
be damned," he said, stroking my cheek with the back of
a hand, looking at the people around us, both stepping
back and holding back, like he didn't really want to.

This wasn't a show for Werner's sake; I could tell the
difference.

For one thing I could see that Nick was trembling
from the inside out, like my being in danger scared the
hell out of him.

It felt good to be cherished, and heck, maybe I should be honored he'd been jealous.

Jaconetti didn't usually expend this much emotion on me or us. We usually let passion rule and emotion be damned. Mostly because we were cowards, but at this moment, there was no hiding feelings, or raw emotion, and it was scary and mind-boggling.

And I liked it.

Werner raised his chin and firmed his spine, indicating that he'd taken responsibility as my rescuer, his pride in the role clear. "Mad's in protective custody," he said. "So now that she has her things, you can all go home secure in the knowledge that she's spending the night protected."

Nick's chin went up, too. "Are you staying?"

"It's my job."

I touched Nick's chin and turned his face my way. "I'll be safe here."

"Well, dammit, ladybug, I let you down. I can protect you."

"You could if she wasn't under arrest and being extradited to New York in the morning."

Nick ran his hand through his hair. "I'd like to ride along in the morning, Detective, if you don't mind?"

Werner became a bit more of a hero in my eyes. "Sure. We'll be leaving at seven."

"I'll be here."

"I'll stay and run the shop," Aunt Fiona said.

"Bless you," I said, hugging her.

My father hooked an arm around my neck. "And whatever I'm doing, I'll also be pacing until you're back, safe."

"Don't worry, Harry, when you're not teaching, I'll keep you busy," Aunt Fee promised.

Nick caught my eye at that, and I tried hard to look noncommittal.

So, now we all knew what Aunt Fiona and my father didn't know—they were a couple; they just didn't know it yet—especially not my father, whose stubborn denial had been known to last for years.

After Nick and my family left, Billings returned with enough Dos Equis and Mexican food to feed the entire night shift.

By two A.M., however, Werner and I were too tired to do anything but nod, so he took my air mattress to a cell, attached the bicycle pump thingy, and blew it up.

After I changed into my jammies and returned to my unlocked cell, I saw that Werner had changed into sweats and socks, and blown up another mattress in the cell adjoining mine.

"I keep overnight provisions, here," he said. "In case."

"So I'm not the first perp you feel the need to keep this close an eye on?"

"Sorry about putting you in a cell." He indicated the squad room and mouthed, "Better than us alone in my office."

I rolled my eyes. "Heaven forbid. The town would

never stop talking about it. Dolly might have a coronary with a piece of gossip that juicy."

Werner came to the bars between us and wrapped his hand around one bar on each side of his face. Son of a stitch, did that make him look vulnerable. He curled a come hither finger my way.

I went and struck the same pose, my hands below his on the bars. "What?" I whispered.

"No matter what happens tomorrow, promise me you'll be careful."

I looked him in the eyes and knew for once he was being serious. "I will."

Werner nodded, turned around, and got comfortable on his mattress.

"Thanks," he said softly.

I thought we'd both toss and turn half the night, but in seconds, Werner was out cold, making those baby porker noises I remembered.

Some guard.

The next thing I knew, he was shaking my shoulder, telling me it was my turn to shower.

Evidently, the night crew cleaned the showers to a power shine for me. I found two guards outside and brand-new yellow plush towels inside.

Afterward, in Werner's office, with the door locked, I changed into my "reading of the will outfit," a long-sleeved, square-necked Valentino, circa 1940. I complimented the dress with a pair of Andre Perugia's 1950s pumps, in black, cream, and gold suede, that Perugia himself said "celebrate the Machine Age." Center top, they had rosette gears, a twisted heel, and black suede toenails.

I smiled, eyes full, looking down at them. The whimsy was my tribute to Dom, who had lusted after these shoes for her own collection.

Now, of course, I wished I'd given them to her.

Hindsight and all that, a waste of energy, like guilt, and the kind of angst over that which cannot be changed.

More than one officer whistled when I exited Werner's office, dressed, made-up, and ready to go, then a minute later, Nick arrived and whistled, too.

"Right on time," Werner said to Nick, as he took my arm.

Talk about poking the tiger. But no, Nick didn't take it that way. He simply took my other arm.

Outside, Kyle and Eve sat waiting in Eve's car to follow us into the city. I should have known that neither of them would let me go through this without them.

My gaze moved between my two hunky escorts, and I wondered what I did to deserve the torture of two such good men vying for my attention, both of whom would protect me to the death.

Both of whom would be considered a great catch.

Both of whom, I would throw back, if I caught one.

Would I? Honestly?

Maybe I was too selfish to share my life.

Maybe after raising my sibs, starting when I was ten,

and ending, well, *never*, I wanted some "me time" for a while.

Maybe if the right one asked . . .

Maybe I needed to see a shrink.

Forty-seven

When you can't do something truly useful, you tend to vent the pent-up energy in something useless but available, like snappy dressing. —LOIS MCMASTER BUJOLD

The drive took several hours, because we got caught up in morning commuter traffic. But Nick got a phone call that seemed interesting from our end.

"Ladybug, good news. They exhumed Victor Pierpont's body. The special agent who looked into Victor's death just told me that Victor didn't die of cancer. The doctor who signed the death certificate has been picked up for questioning. Seems the ME thought there was no need for an autopsy. Victor'd had cancer and the medical examiner's office accepted the doctor's word.

"Now they're working on determining the exact cause of death."

I felt like I'd won a battle, however small, though I hadn't yet, not until Victor's killer was determined.

With Nick and Werner by my side, my extradition to the New York precinct nearest the Pierpont Theater became a mere formality. I never saw a cell or an orange jumpsuit, thank the fashion police.

The rhinestones on the gown proved that I hadn't been in possession of stolen diamonds after all.

All charges were dropped, yay for me, and too bad for the FBI contingent salivating over finding the missing diamonds. Nick looked pretty proud as he regarded his peers with an I-told-you-so smirk on his ungodly handsome face.

When he picked me up and twirled me to celebrate, my heart pretty much went into overdrive, and I rather felt like sneaking him up the getaway tree for my own version of Nick at Night.

Of course, I often felt that way when it was entirely inappropriate and impossible to do anything about it.

We arrived at the DeLong house by ten that morning, Kyle and Eve going off on their own.

As the executor of Dom's will, I was expected to meet with a probate and estate administration attorney before the reading of the will to discuss my role and New York's estate administration process.

Attorney Xavier Yacovone arrived at eleven. I had the mother of all headaches by noon. I had no idea how daunting and time consuming would be my responsibilities as executor.

The good news: Attorney Yacovone had met with Dominique the week before her death, and he had some pretty big aces up his sleeve.

I wondered whether Dom had a death wish or a psychic gift of her own.

I took Nick and Werner into Dom's study and shut the door after I said good-bye to Attorney Yacovone. "Can you arrange to have a couple of FBI agents and plainclothes police present at the reading of the will at four o'clock?"

"That's highly irregular," Werner said.

"Why do you want them?" Nick asked.

"Let's just say that, hopefully, the will could shed some light on the murder investigations, Dom's and Victor's."

"Let me make a few calls," Nick said, leaving as Kyle came into the room.

Kyle, with Eve and I beside him, greeted the people who had been invited to the reading.

All hoping for a honking bequest, the Parasites arrived one by one: Quinny Veneble in a Chanel suit came alone. Ian DeLong in Armani, like he wasn't chasing me all over Mystick Falls last night, came in on the arm of Galina Lockhart in Balenciaga, and their love child, Ursula Uxbridge, the new hands-down hit of *Diamond Sands*, wearing Marc Jacobs.

Pierce Pierpont arrived wearing a six-thousand-dollar Brioni suit with at least a seven-karat single diamond set in chunky soft gold, the nearly pure stuff.

The thing about their expensive clothes was that the

greedy vultures were expecting oodles of money from Dom's estate.

Evidently Zachary, the Wings deliveryman, and every-one who worked on *Diamond Sands*, had been invited. I didn't know half of the theater crew, but Kyle and Pier-pont did.

There was also a large contingent of domestic help, which included Phoebe Muir, Dom's girl Friday; Kerri O'Day, her maid; Rainbow Joy, makeup artist/hair-dresser; Higgins, butler/driver; and Zander Pollock, chef, and the lesser known—to me—household staff.

When two men in suits showed, Nick came over and introduced them to me and Kyle as lawyers in Yaco-vone's firm, but we knew they were FBI.

The police, three of them, simply nodded and walked in, no introductions necessary, though I recognized Buzz and Shinola from the forensics morgue. The cops separated and stood near the doorways while the Feds hung together.

Sure, I knew who put the peanuts in the glue used to bond the diamonds to Dominique's face, which is what killed her during her final curtain call. But my psycho-metric visions would mean nothing in a court of law.

Somehow, I had to get the facts out there during this afternoon's proceedings, and I didn't know if Attorney Yacovone had enough bombshells in his arsenal to pull it off.

Forty-eight

All I want is the best of everything and there's very little of
that left.   —CECIL BEATON

❧

Attorney Yacovone began by introducing himself as an
estate lawyer, and me as Dominique's executor, which
meant that my duties were administrative. They began
with Dom's death and would continue until the estate's
assets had been distributed according to the will. His job
would be seeing the will through probate.

That said, he began with the smaller bequests.

Some of the staff and theater people I didn't know got
$10,000 each. Some seemed sincerely pleased and grate-
ful, others looked and acted like they'd been gypped.

Some got nothing, and their attitudes explained why.

Attorney Yacovone leafed through the will. "Now for
this second section, most of the rest of the household staff,
Ms. DeLong's personal staff, and the cast and crew of *Dia-*

mond Sands can go . . . with the exception of Alfred Higgins, Pierce Pierpont, Phoebe Muir, and Rainbow Joy."

The attorney watched people file out, and he remained silent until the door closed. "Mr. Pierpont, Mr. Ian DeLong, and Mr. Kyle DeLong, this part of the will concerns you."

Ian grinned, the ass, nodded at Galina, and stood at the side of the room toward the front.

Pierce Pierpont sat straighter.

Kyle's throat worked as he reached for Eve's hand.

"My assistant is bringing this item of interest up on the computer, because we'll need it in a minute. All set, Jed?"

The paralegal nodded.

"I'll let you know when we need it. Now please keep in mind, ladies and gentlemen, how determined Ms. DeLong was that I relate this information at this point in the proceedings.

"Kyle DeLong is aware of the information I'm about to impart. His mother shared that with him at the time her will was altered. Please remember that I'm reading this in Dominique's words. 'Friends and parasites: I met the man I would love until the end of my days some time after my husband, Ian DeLong, and my former friend, Galina Lockhart, had an affair and brought their daughter Ursula into the world.' "

Galina screamed, Ursula gasped, and Ian put his fist through the wall. Nobody moved to do a thing about his bloody fist.

" 'Victor Pierpont,' Ms. DeLong goes on to say, 'is

255

the father of my son, Kyle.'" The attorney looked up. "Jed, the computer?"

There was Kyle's birth certificate flashed on the flat screen TV for everyone to see.

"Ugh!" Ursula said. "I used to think that my half brother was *cute*!"

"Thank you, I think," Kyle said, looking at Ursula both surprised and repulsed.

"He's not your half brother," I said, thinking I'd been right, she *wouldn't* be able to spell "motive" if her life depended on it. "Ian is not his father."

"Thank God," Ursula said, and I half expected her to snap her bubble gum.

"Mr. Pierpont, as you can count, you must realize that *your* half brother Kyle is your father's eldest son. That information notwithstanding, it was your father's and Ms. DeLong's initial intention to leave the company in your care, so as not to disrupt company stock and hurt the shareholders. But since you fought to separate them in every way imaginable, the couple married without your knowledge and interference." Yacovone nodded at his assistant. "Jed?"

There it was, Dom's and Victor's marriage license, dated two years before, and signed by a priest from a New York City church, witnessed by Phoebe Muir and Alfred Higgins.

"'For their service to me,' Ms. DeLong states, 'I leave Alfred Higgins and Phoebe Muir each a quarter of a million dollars, and a vice presidency in DeLong Ltd.'"

Ian put another hole in the wall.

Kyle stood. "Officers, if you would be so kind as to restrain that man?"

Ian swore a blue streak when they did.

"Attorney Yacovone," I said, "please explain what Ms. DeLong's marriage means to Mr. Pierce Pierpont."

"I have a note here from Ms. DeLong for Mr. Pierpont." He picked it up. " 'Dear Pierce. Your father and I chose not to go public with our marriage so as not to rock the company boats, both Pierpont Diamond Mines and DeLong Ltd. We had our images to protect. Playful, free, eternal partygoers. That image spoke about our lives and the lives of those who bought our products. It suited us, this mating game of ours. We loved a party where we danced for the public, then went home secretly together. That was, for us, pure marital bliss.

" 'I could have gone public when your father passed. I could have taken the diamond mines away from you, then, but I gave you a chance to redeem yourself. Then I didn't like what I saw and the horror I began to suspect. As the wife of Victor Pierpont, I am now claiming the diamond mines and leaving the company to my son, Kyle DeLong Pierpont, the name my son will soon legally hold.' "

Pierce Pierpont went wild, swearing, furious and mad in the truest sense of the word.

The police stepped in and restrained him, too.

"What are you doing?" Pierce shouted. "I'll have your badges for this!"

"Mr. Pierpont," Attorney Yacovone said. "Dr. Barkley Simmons, the oncologist you paid to falsify your father's death certificate, has confessed to taking your bribe. He admitted that he showed you how to inject a deadly amount of insulin into your father to end his life. He is, what we call in the business, an eyewitness, and he's turned state's evidence."

The police cuffed Pierpont while he looked daggers Kyle's way.

"Pierce," I said. "Don't forget your coat." I threw the black Armani trench coat at him, the coat he wore when he saw Dom switch the jars of body glue, before he gave away her suspicion to the others and arranged for the jars to be switched, again.

"Pierce Pierpont," one of the officers said, "you're under arrest for the murder of Victor Pierpont. You have the right to remain silent . . ."

Pierce's face went a deep ruddy red. "The hell you say!"

Forty-nine

The first time you see everything put together you finally say, "Oh my God, it works!" Because it has been a long process, when it is finished you think, "Finally, it is done!"

—VIVIENNE TAM

❧

I stood up and faced the group. "Before we go any further with the reading of the will, I asked Attorney Yacovone for his indulgence. And if you'd all bear with me, I'll try to make my intentions clear."

I went to stand before Rainbow Joy, who I'd psychically envisioned being coerced into participating in Dominique's murder, because I wore her robe by accident, or by universal design, or by Dom's design.

Rainbow, the ace up my sleeve, had had tears falling down her cheeks through this whole procedure. She trembled when I stopped in front of her. Yes!

"Rainbow, you were the first one to get to Dom after she collapsed onstage. Will you please tell us what happened?"

She began to weep. "When the curtain closed, I saw how purple, blotchy, and painful Dominique's face looked, so I took the diamonds off her to relieve her pain, but there were people all around us and I don't know what happened to the diamonds."

"I'm more interested in why you took the diamonds off her, first thing, no glass of water, no cool towel for what looked like a burn . . ."

"She was in so much pain, and she couldn't breathe."

"Why couldn't she breathe?"

"Because she was allergic to peanuts."

"Before you say anything more," I warned Rainbow, "you should know that Dominique intended for you to have the same bequest as Phoebe and Higgins, but you and I both know why you shouldn't get it, don't we?"

Rainbow shook her head and covered her face with her hands.

I watched the other three murderers: Ian, Galina, and Lance Taggart. Tense faces, sneers, tics. Straight backs. Held breaths.

"What happened to her, Rainbow, to Dominique, the woman who thought of you as a daughter? You didn't want to do it, did you?"

Rainbow glanced up at me then with a questioning look.

"You think people don't talk?" I asked. "You think they don't try to point fingers to take the blame away from themselves?"

Okay, so I was lying. For a good cause.

"I warned you to go back to Connecticut!" Rainbow snapped.

"I know you did with a frightening phone call." I caught Werner's eye. "Tell me what happened, Rainbow. Dom deserved better than she got, especially from you."

Rainbow wiped her face and told us every detail: about being coerced, her head being pushed down and forward by Ian, about the peanuts being left in the body glue overnight for their oily poison to taint the glue, then how they sorted it into small, lethal jars the next morning for spares and for Dominique to use that night. Rainbow also told us who else participated in the plan to put peanuts in Dom's body glue.

Ursula fainted when her mother's name was mentioned. Each of the other murderers, Ian, Dom's ex; Galina, her rival; and Lance, her leading man; got cuffed as Rainbow named them.

"What do you think happened to the diamonds?" I asked Rainbow.

"I can fill in one puzzle piece," Nick said as Rainbow got cuffed, as well. "Gregor Zukovski caught wind of the plan, kept his mouth shut, had an ambulance ready, grabbed what he thought were the diamonds, and had friends of his pretend to be paramedics and move Dominique to the ambulance. That was their getaway," Nick said.

"Zukovski was working independently of the murderers. The rest of them expected Galina to put the diamonds on Dom's seafoam gown and mail it to you, Mad."

I focused on Galina. "Why didn't you tell your partners, the three people with whom you were going to split the value of those diamonds, that they'd disappeared before you could affix them to the seafoam gown?"

"They're murderers," she said.

"So you were afraid for your life?"

"Of course."

"Guess what?" I said. "You're a murderer, too. And you're going to prison for a long time. No diamond cigar bands in there, Ms. Lockhart."

"Do you think they'll give us each a quarter of a sentence," Galina asked, "since we each put a quarter of the poison in?"

Attorney Yacovone looked at her over his glasses. "I'd like to be there when you ask your lawyer that question."

I could barely look at the people who took my friend's life. "Pierce's motive for killing his father was greed. He wanted to own the diamond mines. He didn't want his father to marry, because if he did, his stepmother would get the mines. Makes sense. But the four of you; what did Dom ever do to you?"

"Happy," Ian said through clenched teeth. "She was so damned happy all the time—" He stopped and looked around.

"And you wanted to wipe that smile off her face and get your hands on her half of your partnership," I said. "Jealousy and greed."

"As for the others, Dom's part in *Diamond Sands* might have gone to you, Galina, right?"

"It was promised to me."

"Rainbow, what did you do, get caught up in the excitement, the glamour? Different from being the daughter of flower children, wasn't it?"

The girl nodded and lowered her head.

"Lance, you're a puzzle," I said.

"I want my lawyer," Lance Taggart said.

"Dom didn't return your affection, did she? You weren't used to being rebuffed. Ever."

"It was all Taggart's idea," Ian shouted. "He slobbered all over Dom when he was drunk, and he's hated her since she and Victor maligned his manhood in public one night."

Lance Taggart scoffed at Ian. "Yes, and Ian, that was the night you proposed this scheme, but I see now that you had a lot more to gain than we did."

Then you're stupid for not seeing it sooner, I thought.

Galina backed up Taggart's statement that they started to hatch their plan the night of that particular party. "Dom wasn't particularly friendly to any of us that night. It was all Victor, Victor, Victor."

Kyle shook his head. "I remember that party. They'd just found out that my father, Victor, was cancer free. No wonder they had eyes only for each other."

Nick approached the perps. "It was you, Taggart, who broke into my house, or tried to, on three separate occasions, looking for the seafoam gown and diamonds, right?"

"Lawyer," Lance said.

"I figured," I admitted, "that Taggart went looking for the gown after Phoebe and Zachary took the train back here from Mystic, right, Lance? And Ian, you followed Werner and me to the police station last night after the fashion show because I had the gown. It was stupid of you, by the way, to jump up to catch the rhinestones like that."

"Rhinestones? Damn it," Ian snapped. "Then who got the diamonds?"

"Nobody knows," I said. "Dominique wore cubic zirconias to do her last show and Zukovski got them."

Attorney Yacovone cleared his throat. "If you'll all be patient and wait to discuss loose threads later, like the location of the diamonds, there are only two bequests left."

The police waited, their prisoners cuffed, and I sat down. "Proceed," I said.

"Thank you, Miss Cutler. This is also in Ms. DeLong's words: 'I leave all my worldly possessions to my son, Kyle, except for my doll collection, which I leave to my dear friend, Madeira Cutler.'" The attorney stood and packed his briefcase. "That's my part in the proceedings done."

"Now *that* I hadn't expected," I said as he left. "Dom left me her fashion dolls and her Velvalee Dickenson dolls?"

"The dolls," Kyle said. "And everything in them."

Werner frowned. "What's a Velvalee Dickinson doll?"

"During World War II, Velvalee Dickinson had a doll shop here in New York on Madison Avenue. A spy for Japan, she used to ship the dolls with coded messages in them giving away United States secrets. They called her the Doll Woman after she was convicted of espionage and went to prison for seven years. Dom and I both collected her dolls, among other fashion dolls. Velvalee owns an unenviable place in the history of World War II, but her dolls were beautiful."

I went to the cabinet, shook each doll, and found two that were not empty. I brought them to Kyle. "May I?"

"They're yours," he said, "as is anything inside."

I took the first doll apart and caught a handful of bling. "The diamonds." I looked at them shining in my hand, opened Kyle's fist, and let them fall like twinkling stars from my palm into his. "Your mother sparkled like that inside and out. Sell them and split the money between the Keep Me Foundation and St. Anthony's in your mother's name."

"That's extraordinarily generous of you, Mad, but do you understand how much money you're giving away?"

"Dominique died for those diamonds. They have to do some good to redeem themselves."

"I think she died to avenge my father's death," Kyle said, "but we'll never know. And given this turn of events,

Mad, you've solved a big problem for me. Mom's vintage clothing collection. I can't go through the agony of selling it, and I can't bear having it around. It's yours. Do what you want with it. I know she wanted you to have Coco's dress, anyway."

"Coco's dress belongs in a museum, also in your mother's name. I'll take care of it."

"Thanks, Sis." Kyle hugged me.

"What dress couldn't you find," I asked him, "that was supposed to go to me? You mentioned it that first day."

"I made that up for Ian's benefit. He would have been too nosy about why you were here and involved, otherwise. Bottom line, Mom trusted you to see that justice was done."

I sighed. "I just don't understand why your mother didn't go to the police when she thought she was in danger," I said, not for the first time.

An officer stepped forward. "Ms. DeLong tried. She messengered a tainted jar of diamond glue to us, smudged fingerprints and all. But the messenger got into an accident, the package fell apart, and it took several days to reach us. Bottom line: She probably thought she was temporarily safe after having switched jars of body glue. If we'd gotten it the day she sent it, she might, or might not, be alive today."

My heart in my throat, I opened the second doll, took out two notes, read them silently, and handed them to Kyle.

He gave them back to me. "Read them out loud, Mad."

I stood. "This one's quite short," I said. *"To the Parasites: I do so like getting even."*

I put that note down for the longer one, the one to me.

"Dearest Mad, I tried to save myself, but I lost my joie de vivre and the heart to fight when I lost Victor. Please know that there was nothing that either of us could have done.

"You know that I wouldn't have liked getting old, but I don't much mind dying before my career died, or of going out young, vibrant, and dancing in the Summerland with Victor.

"You know me, always a grand finale.

"Thank you my friend. Live long and happy.

"Brightest Blessings.

"Love, Dom."

Kyle touched his BlackBerry and Dominique's smooth rich voice comforted us, despite our tears.

"I've sung the grand finale, traveled some amazing byways, and so much fun for me . . . I sang it my way."

A Lesson in
Fake Designer Handbags

❧

I bought a used Prada handbag as my vintage bag this time around, because it's a lovely, olive retro design, and I knew my daughter would love it. I also suspected that, since it was a bargain, it might not be the real thing.

But I also thought that this would be a good lesson to all of us, if I researched it and learned if it was a fake and why, so you'd know what to look for in a designer bag that you don't buy new from a department store.

First of all it's shaped something like a wide-open fan, like Regency ladies used to flirt with. Take the fan design and cut the point off about half way up, and you have the shape of my "Prada" bag.

You can see mine on my website at www.annetteblair .com/vintage_magic_handbags.htm.

Why do I believe mine's a fake? First of all, it doesn't have antique brass hardware, which all Pradas do, I've learned. Mine has a silver zipper. First clue.

Second, the lining, while lovely, doesn't have the word "Prada" embroidered all over it, though there is a fair imitation of a Prada emblem embossed on the top front of the bag, with the word "Milano" beneath it and an escutcheon too small to see.

Third, the seams inside are not invisible.

Fourth, the straps are too thin, though they're smart looking and attached to black ovals on the bag, which adds to its lovely retro look.

Inside my bag there is another, smaller version of itself, same color, without the retro straps, though it does have a shoulder strap hooked to it with removable hooks in silver. You can call it a clutch or change purse if you will. It could serve either purpose.

There you have the story of my "Prada" bag.

I wish you happy vintage bag hunting of your own and a specimen of high quality that's the real thing.

Turn the page for a preview of
Annette Blair's next book
in the Vintage Magic Mysteries . . .

Skirting the Grave

Coming soon from Berkley Prime Crime!

I want a big house with a moat and dragons and a fort to keep people out!
　　　　　　　　　　　　　　　　　　—VICTORIA BECKHAM

⚜

Eve breezed into my shop. "Mad," she said. "I just heard that Nick's coming home. Did you ever confess to that thermonuclear kiss you shared with Werner the night you two slept together?"

I growled. Yes, growled, like a big cat. An angry cat. "We did *not* sleep together! We were out cold, both of us concussed . . . in the same bed. There's a difference."

"But the kiss did happen. You couldn't both have dreamed it."

"Get out, Meyers!"

Eve gave me that knowing grin of hers. "You didn't tell the boy toy, did you?"

"He's been on assignment the entire two months. The

273

FBI takes advantage of their agents like that. I haven't seen him since."

"What?" she asked. "You lost Nick's cell phone number?"

"He changed it."

Eve grinned. "Hah! Is he ever pouting."

"No kidding," I snapped, Nick being only one of my problems.

Eve's watch alarm rang. "Gotta run. Class in twenty."

"See you later, then." I hung my "Out to Lunch" sign and shut and locked the door. I needed control over my life and that was the best I could manage on short notice.

Dante Underhill, my Cary Grant–type ghost, regarded me as if I might need to talk and he'd be willing to listen.

"Give me a quiet half hour first," I said.

His chin dimple deepened with his worry lines, and he disappeared.

Peace. I reveled in it as I stretched out on the fainting couch and closed my eyes. The scent of chocolate curled around me. My mother had been gone twenty years and was still reaching out to me. The more of her mystical, magical gifts I discovered in myself, the nearer she seemed.

So what's my problem?

Brandy, my phantom sister, is due home anytime now, and she's set me up as neatly as if she'd tied my wrists and ankles together.

In the same way that I, Madeira Cutler, am my mother's daughter, psychic abilities and all, my sister Brandy—third Cutler, second daughter—resembles . . . no one. While Brandy denies the existence of my metaphysical gifts and scoffs at my love of vintage fashion, she's not beyond soliciting my wealthy clients to seed her worthy cause, which will require a lot of work in the next couple of weeks . . . on *my* part.

Where my father, the English professor, quotes literary greats, Brandy quotes philanthropists and world hunger organizations. I admire her for that and for giving up her eternal stint in the peace corps to raise money for a good cause. Guess where she's starting? Here in Mystic.

To be fair, she planned her fundraising trip to coincide with our sister Sherry's baby shower. Justin Vancortland IV, Sherry's father-in-law, is lending us his mansion for Brandy's events. She and Cort shared barbs at Sherry's wedding, and he gave her a donation. Better than good cooking as a way to Brandy's heart.

Don't get me wrong. I've missed my sister. But she didn't just force a few fundraisers on me, she also talked me into taking on a design assistant. An unpaid one, it's true, and on the plus side, Isobel Yost, or Izzy, as Brandy calls her, is practically paying me to take her on by giving me her grandmother's vintage clothes, which I might or might not accept, depending on her attachment to them.

It seems Izzy applied for several fashion design reality shows and never quite made it. She wants to learn at the feet of a master. That's the crap Brandy handed me, anyway. Fact is, I agreed because Izzy works for a top modeling agency and she's getting her wealthy boss, Madame Celine Robear, to attend the fundraiser, a coup for Brandy in her new role as development director for the Nurture Kids Foundation. Besides, I need the models Madame Celine is bringing for the fashion show.

My cell phone rang, and since I was beginning to think my problems weren't that huge, I answered it.

"Mad," Brandy said. "Izzy and I aren't coming in on the same train after all. There was a mix-up and she'll be in before me, like maybe five minutes ago? Can you pick her up at the train station?"

Now I remembered why I thought things could get out of hand. "I'm on my way," I said, clapping my phone shut before I growled or gave her a bit of snark.

Mystic's train station projected a quaint landmark beauty. Small and full of character, painted cream, its detailed architectural trim a rusty orange, it had once been used as a model for a toy train terminal by American Flyer. In minutes, I parked in the lot. On the track side, I saw no passengers. They only got off at the station if they were going south.

As the northbound train disappeared around the curve, its absence revealed a swarm of motion. People dragging bags around an ambulance parked on the cross street with its bubble light turning. Directly across from the station, a humming crowd faced into the lean-to where people waited in bad weather.

A compelling whiff of chocolate hit me, and I ran, my heart racing. It couldn't be Brandy. I broke through the crowd to find a girl passed out on the bench, a paramedic checking her vitals, and I ignored my shiver of unease. Nearby stood Detective Sergeant Lytton Werner, or "Little Wiener" as I'd dubbed him in third grade. Call ours a grudging relationship, except when awareness sizzled, as it unfortunately had one scary night.

Werner gave me a double take. "Madeira, don't tell me you know this girl?"

"No, I was afraid it was Brandy." Relief flooded my senses. "I'm here to pick up my new assistant." I looked back at the terminal, shading my eyes from the April sun to see if someone looked lost. "Isobel Yost," I said, glancing back at Werner, his lips firming. "Has anybody seen her?"

Werner took my arm to walk me away from the crowd, and I knew. "That's her," he said. "She's dead, Mad. I'm sorry."

GET CLUED IN

Ever wonder how to find out about all the latest Berkley Prime Crime and Signet mysteries?

berkleyobsidianmysteries.com

- *See what's new*
- *Find author appearances*
- *Win fantastic prizes*
- *Get reading recommendations*
- *Sign up for the mystery newsletter*
- *Chat with authors and other fans*
- *Read interviews with authors you love*

MYSTERY SOLVED.

berkleyobsidianmysteries.com

M2G0808

"[Features a] spunky heroine and sparkling wit."
—Kerrelyn Sparks,
New York Times bestselling author

FIFTH IN THE PEPPER MARTIN MYSTERIES

DEAD MAN TALKING

CASEY DANIELS

Author of *Tomb with a View*

Heiress-turned-cemetery-tour-guide Pepper Martin is
not happy to discover that a local reality TV show,
Cemetery Survivor, will be filmed at Cleveland's Mon-
roe Street Cemetery—and she has to be a part of it. To
make matters worse, the ghost of a wrongly convicted
killer needs Pepper's help to clear his name. But digging for the truth could put her in grave danger.

penguin.com

M649T0210

Cozy up with
Berkley Prime Crime

SUSAN WITTIG ALBERT
Don't miss the national bestselling
series featuring herbalist China Bayles.

LAURA CHILDS
The Tea Shop Mysteries are the
toast of Charleston, South Carolina.

KATE KINGSBURY
The Pennyfoot Hotel Mystery
series is a teatime delight.

For the armchair
detective in you.

penguin.com

M6G0708